Girl Geeks

GIRLGEEKACADEMY

presents

Written by Alex Miles

PUFFIN BOOKS

PUFFIN BOOKS

UK | USA | Canada | Ireland | Australia
India | New Zealand | South Africa | China

Penguin Random House Australia is part of the Penguin Random House group of
companies whose addresses can be found at global.penguinrandomhouse.com.

First published by Puffin Books, an imprint of Penguin Random House Australia Pty Ltd,
in 2019

Cover design by Amanda Watts
Cover and illustrations by Taieri Christopherson
Typeset in 15/23 pt Adobe Garamond Pro by Midland Typesetters, Australia

Printed and bound in Australia by Griffin Press, part of Ovato, an accredited
ISO AS/NZS 14001 Environmental Management Systems printer

A catalogue record for this
book is available from the
National Library of Australia

ISBN 978 0 14 379506 3

Penguin Random House Australia uses papers that are natural and recyclable products,
made from wood grown in sustainable forests. The logging and manufacture processes are
expected to conform to the environmental regulations of the country of origin.

penguin.com.au

Girl Geek Academy acknowledges Australia's First Nations Peoples as the Traditional
Owners and Custodians of the land and gives respect to the Elders – past and present –
and through them to all Aboriginal and Torres Strait Islander peoples.

For the girl gangs out there who give each other strength in different ways, and my three best boys, Fred, Paul and George – A.M.

What would the internet look like if more women were building it? This book is dedicated to all the women who want to, and those that already are – Amanda, Tammy, Lisy, April and Sarah

Girl gang/gurl gang/ *noun*. **1.** A group of girls who enjoy hanging out together. They have mutual interests but more importantly they have differences – this is how they are stronger together. **2.** Your biggest fans and your own personal cheerleaders. They get excited for your success. **3.** Recognise when you need help – 'my girl gang help each other through the tough times, and encourages me to be the best version of myself'.

Hmmm, Niki pondered as she swiped up on her tablet screen. *Peter Peacock? Niki Newt? Zelda Zebra?* She was inspecting all the character choices in a new game. She'd never played *Cookie Jar Detectives* before. In fact, no one in her class had. And it wasn't every day that you got to do gaming at school.

'I reckon I'll be George the Giraffe,' said Niki's friend, Hamsa. They were sitting at the table by the window in class, along with their other friends Maggie and Eve.

'Peter Peacock for me,' said Maggie, pushing her glasses up along her nose. 'Look at that gorgeous tail.'

'Niki, your choice is obvious, right?' said Eve, pointing at the lizard-looking creature on her screen. 'Having a newt named after you has got to be a sign.'

Hamsa laughed. 'What a weird word – "newt"? I've never heard of them.'

'We saw them sometimes when we went camping in the States,' explained Eve. She'd recently moved back to Australia after living in San Francisco. That was when the girls had become friends. Niki hadn't had much to do with Hamsa and Maggie before then. Not that she didn't like them, they just never realised they had anything in common. But teaming up to build an app in a school Hackathon project had changed all that.

Eve was wearing her long black hair down today. She curled a few strands around her finger as she inspected the character list on her screen. 'Did you know that newts can grow their limbs back if they get chopped off?' she said.

'Wow!' said Maggie.

'Weird!' said Hamsa, with her nose screwed up.

'I'll go the newt,' said Niki. 'The weirder the better.' She was never bothered by what other people thought of her.

Once everyone in class had selected their characters, their teacher, Ms Atlas, went over to the whiteboard. She wrote 'Point of view' in big letters across the top, drawing smiley faces inside each 'o'. 'I bet you're wondering why on earth we're gaming in class, when I said we'd be writing stories.'

Kids around the class nodded while one boy, Ezra, yelled out, 'No complaints here!'

'There's a saying that "there are two sides to every story",' continued Ms Atlas.

Sal, one of Niki's classmates, put her hand up. 'Yeah! Like when my sister screams that I've stolen her new favourite jumper, and I explain I'm only *borrowing* it.'

Ms Atlas laughed. 'Exactly. Stories are different depending on whose point of view you follow. And I want us to think about that when we're writing our own stories.'

Ms Atlas tapped a couple of buttons so the screen of her tablet was displayed on the whiteboard for everyone to see. 'Now that you've chosen your characters, let me explain how *Cookie Jar Detectives* works. It's called a narrative game, and it's kind of like reading a choose-your-own-adventure book – you're

in control, your choices affect the outcome of the story, *and* the story will be different depending on which character you choose.'

Ms Atlas tapped on the peacock. The game zoomed in on the animal, flashing his brightly coloured tail. 'The aim is to discover who stole the cookie from the cookie jar. But beware, each character will tell *their* version of events. Do you think that will lead you to choose a different suspect in the end?'

Ms Atlas tapped her chin with her finger, like a detective deep in thought. Niki loved how playful her teacher was – she had a way of making everything at school interesting.

'All right,' said Ms Atlas, excitedly. 'Ready up, let's go!'

The class were off in a flash and barely anyone spoke as they followed their characters through the game.

Niki was right into the bright animation and thought the background music was a perfect mix of kooky and suspenseful. Her fingers danced across the screen with ease, instructing Niki Newt on what to do next. It wasn't surprising Niki was so fast – she was a pro with anything tech.

'I can't wait to tell Mum we played games in class,' said Niki.

'Why?' asked Eve.

'Because she *hates* them,' said Niki. 'In fact, it's hard to know what my parents hate more – that I'm into gaming . . . or coding . . . or skateboarding.'

Niki glanced over to Hamsa's screen. 'Check it out,' she said. 'Our characters are both in the kitchen, seeing it from different angles.'

All the girls took a closer look. Hamsa's giraffe was so tall she could see the cookie jar on the kitchen bench. Niki Newt, on the other hand, was close to the ground. She couldn't see the bench as the kitchen cupboards towered above her, but she *could* see a tiny trail of crumbs leading to the pantry.

'Legend!' Hamsa said proudly as she pointed at the cookie jar. 'I knew the giraffe was the best character.'

She playfully gave herself a pat on the back. Then she tapped on her screen to walk the giraffe out of the room.

WHACK!

The game made a thumping sound effect followed by birds whistling.

Hamsa looked devastated. 'It says I forgot to duck and hit my head on the doorway. I'm knocked out for three minutes. Now I'm never going to solve this crime!'

Maggie, Niki and Eve couldn't help but laugh.

'How's that giraffe going for you now?' asked Niki with a mischievous smile.

'Yeah, yeah,' said Hamsa, begrudgingly. 'Point taken.'

Chapter 2

When the class had finished playing *Cookie Jar Detectives* they chatted at their tables about how each character's point of view was different, even when they'd witnessed the same thing. When they started to write their own stories, Niki couldn't believe how many words flew out of her pen. She never thought of herself as being great at creative writing, but this exercise just clicked for her somehow.

'Whoa, Niki, slow down. Your hand will fall off writing that fast,' said Eve.

Niki laughed. 'This exercise is fun though.'

'Sure is,' added Maggie.

'Even *I* like it!' said Hamsa. 'And I'm not one of those gaming types.'

'Oh,' said Niki, with her eyebrows raised. 'And what *type* is that?

Hamsa swallowed, like she was trying to work out what to say without offending Niki.

Niki loved watching her squirm. Ever since she and Hamsa had become friends, their favourite thing to do together was argue.

'I actually couldn't care less if you are gamers or not,' said Niki.

'Thanks a lot!' said Hamsa.

'Sorry, I don't mean that in a nasty way. I just mean that it's fine for us to be interested in different stuff.'

Hamsa nodded. That was something she and Niki *could* agree on.

'You know what though,' said Niki, getting an idea. 'If you *are* interested in learning a bit more about gaming, there's a LAN party on this weekend. You should come.'

'A LAN party?' asked Eve.

'It stands for Local Area Network party,' explained Niki. 'It's basically a club where you can meet and play in person, rather than playing online. Universities run them, or LAN cafés like this one coming up, or sometimes people hold them at their houses and you bring along your own consoles or computers.'

'You're not selling the dream here,' said Hamsa.

Niki bit her lip, weighing up how important it was for her to go to the LAN party. She had a group of friends who gamed online together. The other three had met in person before, but not Niki. She was keen to meet them. So Niki did something she hardly ever did.

'Let me ask you as a favour then,' she said, putting her biscuit down and giving the girls her full attention. 'I've been asking my parents for months to go to one of these LAN parties. They always say no, but if you all come too, there's a chance they'll agree.'

'Let me get this straight,' said Hamsa. 'In the presence of Eve Lee, Maggie Milsom and yours truly, Hamsa Pillai . . . Niki Apostolidis is officially asking for help?'

'Just a small favour, but yes, I suppose,' said Niki.

'Well, I never thought we'd see the day,' added Eve, with a wink.

'Please?' said Niki.

Eve, Maggie and Hamsa looked to one another.

'I'm at my dad's this weekend, but I'll ask,' said Maggie.

'C'mon, I'll go if we all go,' said Eve.

They looked at Hamsa.

'Fine,' said Hamsa.

'Yes!' said Niki. 'I promise it'll be fun. The guys I game with will be there too. Well, two of them at least. The other one lives interstate.'

'Have you ever met them?' asked Eve.

'Not in person,' said Niki. 'We play with headsets though, so I've heard all their voices. I don't even know what their real names are. We use our game names when we play, which means I know them as FEARlix, MegaMax and AstroArchie. They only know me as TrickiNiki.'

'TrickiNiki?' said Maggie, giggling. 'I like it.'

'So what are they like?' asked Eve. 'Will we get on with them?'

Niki shrugged. 'Don't see why not.'

'But are they all boys?' asked Hamsa.

Niki nodded and Hamsa slouched back in her chair. She seemed disappointed.

Niki didn't understand what the big deal was. 'Who cares if they're boys,' she said confidently. 'We can all be friends, right?'

'Some people have a totally different persona online versus real life,' said Maggie. 'What if they're crazy?'

'Or boring? Or rude?' added Hamsa.

'Nah, it'll be right,' said Niki. And she wasn't just putting on a front. If she got on well with her gamer friends online, there was no reason why they shouldn't in real life too. Was there?

Chapter 3

'It looks like a regular café to me,' said Eve. She was waiting with Maggie, Niki and Niki's mum out the front of the LAN café. Inside, there were tables and chairs along one side of the room, a food and drinks counter on the other side, and a bench with stools facing the front window. It was light and airy, with posters plastered across the walls that showcased a mix of the latest release games and retro classics.

Niki's mum, Angela, looked up from her phone. 'Surely not. Just wait until we take a closer look inside,' she said.

15

'Don't knock it till we've tried it, Mum,' said Niki. She wished her parents were more open-minded.

'Do you like gaming, Angela?' asked Eve.

'About as much as I like cutting onions,' said Angela. 'What about you?'

'Never really tried it,' said Eve. 'I mean, I've played games on my tablet before, and my dad's phone, but nothing like this. Niki was pretty convincing when she asked us to come along today.'

'Yes,' said Angela, nodding. 'Convincing others is one of Niki's superpowers.'

Niki forced a smile. She couldn't tell if that was an insult or a compliment. She quickly changed the subject. 'I'm so excited you're all here. I wonder which characters you'll like best.'

'Do we get to choose?' asked Maggie.

'You bet!' said Niki. 'So long as the people you're playing with haven't chosen that character already. They all have different skills and personalities and equipment.'

'Sorry I'm late!' called Hamsa, rushing over to meet the others. Her dad, Roshan, was following behind her.

'It's okay. It looks like we're the first here anyway,' said Niki.

'We're just discussing which characters we'll play,' added Eve.

'Oh, yes!' said Hamsa excited. 'I have to be someone with long spiky hair!'

Niki laughed. 'It's more about what you can *do*, not what you look like, but sure, there's a character with spiky hair.'

Niki led the girls inside and they were greeted by the woman behind the counter. She had straight hair, bleached with purple and pink streaks, and pinned back at one side with a Hello Kitty clip.

'Hi, *ni hao*, *bonjour*!' she said. 'I'm Yumi. First time here?'

'It is for me, her and her,' said Hamsa, pointing at herself, Eve and Maggie. 'And this is Niki – she's a long-time player, first-time LAN party-er.'

'Great to meet you all,' said Yumi. 'Come on through.'

Yumi stepped out from behind the counter and led the girls down the corridor. 'You're early so you've got the place to yourselves for a bit.'

The corridor opened up to reveal a large room with rows of desks. There was a computer set up in front of every chair. The walls were painted black and the lights were dimmed.

'This is more like what I expected,' said Angela. 'Will there be many kids coming today?'

'It'll be a full house,' said Yumi. 'I've been working here for years while studying for my engineering degree. The kids' LAN parties always pack out.'

'It's nice for the kids to meet in person,' said Roshan. 'Rather than only playing in the la-la-land of the internet.'

'Dad!' said Hamsa through gritted teeth, like she was willing him to stop embarrassing her.

'Let's get cracking before Team Jupiter arrive,' said Niki. She was met with blank stares. 'Team Jupiter – it's the name of my gaming team.'

'Why?' asked Maggie.

'AstroArchie chose it. He totally geeks out about astronomy. Anyway, you girls need to

19

practice! I gotta make sure you're not complete noobs.'

There it was again – Eve, Hamsa and Maggie looked like they were lost in space.

'Noobs. You know, like "newbies" . . . new to the game . . . forget it,' said Niki.

She found a nook at the back of the room and the girls all sat nearby. Yumi set them up with their computers and headsets.

'Testing, one, two, three,' said Hamsa, adjusting the volume.

'We can hear you,' said Niki, amused by Hamsa, always wanting to look the part. She noticed Maggie staring at a poster on the wall. 'That's it, Maggie. My favourite game.'

Maggie pointed at the poster. It had 'Castle Capture' written in big letters across the top.

'Great choice,' said Yumi. 'I'm a mega CC fan too. And there's a little something I think you'll be *very* excited about later.'

'What?' asked Niki.

Yumi smiled and covered her lips. 'It's top-secret until everyone arrives.'

'How does the game work?' asked Hamsa.

'It's set in a kind of medieval fantasy world,' said Niki. 'And there are two teams trying to capture the castle. First team with all their players inside, wins.'

'How many players in each team?' asked Maggie.

'As many as you like. That's where strategy comes into it! Bigger isn't always better. If you've got twenty players in your team, you've got more strength, *but* it's also harder to communicate. I reckon four or five players is best.'

'Hold-up, are we the goodies or the baddies here?' asked Hamsa.

'Both I guess,' said Yumi. 'The castle is empty, so both teams have equal right to it. It depends on which character you choose. Some are big and use brute force to help their team win. Others use their brains or have special equipment.'

'It takes all types to make a good team,' added Niki. 'That's why I love this game so much. It's different every time you play it, depending on which characters are in your team, and who's in the opposition. Half the battle is working out your strengths and weaknesses, finding a strategy and communicating with each other.'

Angela and Roshan watched on as Niki helped the girls choose their characters. Maggie chose Sheryl, a warrior princess who could walk on rainbows. Eve went for Ruffleous, a fire-breathing baby dragon. He couldn't talk to humans, which made communication difficult, but he could smell danger when the opposition were nearby so that definitely made up for it.

Hamsa was disappointed to see the only spiky haired character was Electrica, a farm girl who'd been struck by lightning and now had the power to shoot lightning bolts out of her hair.

'I don't like her outfit,' said Hamsa.

'Electrica is awesome, I'll play her,' offered Niki. 'There's a unicorn called Unique who can –'

'Say no more! I'm in,' said Hamsa.

The girls got started, making plenty of mistakes and having plenty of laughs. Even though they didn't have another team to compete with, they were able to play against the computer and each game took around twenty minutes. They were so into it they barely looked up from their screens, and didn't even notice the other players arriving.

It wasn't until Unique fell off the drawbridge and was waiting to be rescued that a bored Hamsa looked around the room.

'Ahh, ladies,' Hamsa whispered into her headset. 'I think we're the only girls here.'

'So?' said Niki, firing another lightning bolt.

Hamsa stood up and surveyed the room, before quickly retreating to her chair. 'It's official. One hundred per cent stinky boys.'

'How do you know they stink?' asked Eve, moving her character forward as there was the scent of trouble nearby.

'I have four brothers,' said Hamsa. 'I'm an expert on boy pong.'

'Just wait until we meet my team,' said Niki. 'They'll be fine.'

When their game finished Yumi called everyone into the front of the café. Niki and the girls stuck close together. It seemed like some of the boys were already friends, but the majority stood on their own or with their parents.

'Welcome, *bienvenido, hwan-yeong*,' said Yumi, standing on one of the chairs so everyone could see her. 'Today is all about making friends and having fun. If you see someone alone, introduce yourself, either with your game name or your real name. I, for example, am Yumi, but you can also call me Catlady13.'

There were hushed giggles from around the room. Niki scanned the faces, trying to work out who AstroArchie and MegaMax were.

'In many ways, LAN parties are retro,' said Yumi. 'When I was your age it was the only way to get together for multiplayer games. Nowadays, even though you can play together online, there's something special about an old-school meet-up.'

Niki agreed. She was always curious about how people could be different online compared to real life.

'In exciting news,' said Yumi. 'I bet you all know the Castle Capture Cup is coming to town.'

Niki nodded, along with every kid in the room . . . except for Hamsa, Maggie and Eve who looked more confused than a Pokémon under a Paralysis move.

'It's a stadium-sized, televised national esports tournament and I can officially be the first to tell you that this year there'll be a category just for kids!'

'No way!' squealed Niki.

'How do we enter?' shouted one boy.

'Where do we buy tickets?' called another.

'Can we dress as our favourite characters?' someone else wanted to know.

'Details will be available online later today,' shouted Yumi over all the questions. 'How about we get some practice in.'

There was a stampede down the corridor as the players couldn't wait to get started. Niki and the girls were rushed along in the wave.

'I don't get it,' said Eve 'Why is this such a big deal?'

'There are hardly any comps for kids,' explained Niki as they went into the room. 'Competing in something like this is a huge deal. It'll feel like the Olympics for gaming.'

'I wonder how many players will be in a team?' asked a boy walking behind Niki.

Niki turned around to answer. 'With a tournament it has to be four players.'

The boy, who was tall, with shaggy brown hair, looked at her as if to say, 'I wasn't asking you', so Niki turned around and kept walking.

'Imagine if our team competed together,' said another boy behind them. 'You, me, FEARlix and TrickiNiki.'

Niki spun back around at the mention of her name.

'What?' asked the tall boy rudely.

'It's me! I'm TrickiNiki.'

Niki threw her arms around the other boy, hugging him quickly. He was frozen like a statue. 'You're TrickiNiki?' he said, sounding confused.

The tall boy seemed even more perplexed. 'I thought your name was Nick,' he insisted. 'And that you'd be, um . . .'

'A boy?' asked Niki, folding her arms in front her herself, just below the slogan on her t-shirt that read: 'It's cool to be kind'. 'Let me guess, you're MegaMax?'

The tall boy huffed. 'How'd you know?'

Niki shrugged her shoulders casually. 'I thought you'd be . . .'

'Full of yourself?' Hamsa whispered to Eve, who tried to hide her laughter.

'Tall,' said Niki. 'Or super short. Because of your name.'

She turned to the other boy. He was wearing cuffed jeans and a jumper with the iconic Apollo 11 moon landing printed on it. 'You must be Archie.'

'Yeah, sorry about before. It's great to meet you TrickiNiki,' he said. 'Max and I go to school together. And Felix, or "FEARlix" is my cousin. And sorry again, but what *is* your name?'

'I'm Niki,' she said. 'It's great to meet you too. These are my school friends, Hamsa, Eve and Maggie.'

The girls waved shyly and Niki wished they were more outgoing. 'They're noobs, should we show them how it's done?' she said, trying to make the girls feel part of the team.

'For sure,' said Archie. He followed Niki along a row of desks, with Max following grumpily behind. Meeting her teammates wasn't quite what she'd expected, but surely Max would get over himself soon enough.

Chapter 4

 TEAM JUPITER – VOICE CHAT ENABLED

🖊 **TrickiNiki:**
FEARlix, we missed you yesterday at the LAN party.

🐱 **FEARlix:**
I know. It sucks living so far away.

🦖 **MegaMax:**
Did you catch up on the big news?
TrickiNiki is a girl!

🐱 **FEARlix:**
Um, yeah, Archie told me. Hi, Niki.

TrickiNiki:
I can't believe you bozos couldn't tell
from my voice.

MegaMax:
What do you mean?

TrickiNiki:
Hello, do I sound like a boy to you?

MegaMax:
Well, um, I guess now that we know
you're a girl, you do sound like one.

AstroArchie:
Is your real name Nicole?

TrickiNiki:
Nikoleta, but everyone calls me Niki.
I can still be TrickiNiki to you guys though.

> **New opponent has joined the
> game – Magic10**

> **Magic10 would like to chat to you
> ACCEPT / DECLINE**

> **TrickiNiki declined the invitation**

TrickiNiki:
Buzz off Magic10. It's creepy chatting to complete strangers.

MegaMax:
Creepy. And my parents would ban me from playing if I did that.

FEARlix:
Mine too. This Magic10 guy's playing Myke the mouse. I've never played that character before.

💰 **MegaMax collects 20,000 gold coins**

TrickiNiki:
Great job, Max.

MegaMax:
Thanks, Nikoleta.

AstroArchie:
I reckon the tower on the south wall is empty, should we head there?

TrickiNiki:
It'll be a trap. Let's hold out here. Remember that boat we found the other

day that took us to the secret entrance in the moat? FEARlix, use your diving spell to find it and, MegaMax, you could try a summoning enchantment.

🦖 **MegaMax:**
Sounds good, Nikoleta.

🦎 **TrickiNiki:**
Stop calling me that.

🦖 **MegaMax:**
Okay, Nikoleta, I'll stop . . . Seriously, I'll stop now for real.

🏰 **Magic10 has entered the castle**

🚀 **AstroArchie:**
WHAT!?

🦖 **MegaMax:**
At least he's the only one through. I can see the rest of his team on the west wall.

🦎 **TrickiNiki:**
Okay, new plan. AstroArchie, use your smoke cloud so FEARlix can sneak

34

through the same entrance undetected. And FEARlix, save your ultimate. You'll need it inside.

🚀 **AstroArchie:**
On it.

🐱 **FEARlix:**
Me too.

🦖 **MegaMax:**
Who is this Magic10, anyway? I can't believe he got past us.

🛹 **TrickiNiki:**
He or she?!

🦖 **MegaMax:**
HE obviously. There's no way a girl could be that good. Unless she's stolen her brother's account like TrickiNiki did.

💰 **Magic10 found 20,000 gold coins**

🦖 **MegaMax:**
Oh, come on, I'm joking guys . . . it is kind of funny.

🚀 AstroArchie:
No, it's not Max. Leave her alone.

🦖 MegaMax:
What!? Niki's one of us. She can take a joke.

🚀 AstroArchie:
It's a dumb joke. And anyway we should be –

⚔️ **FEARlix has been trapped**

🐱 FEARlix:
Sorry! I made it in, but there was a giant spider. It's spun me into a web and I can't get out.

🚀 AstroArchie:
Niki . . . You still there?

✏️ TrickiNiki:
Yep. FEARlix, I told you you'd need your ultimate. Don't worry. We're coming to save you. Max, get in position.

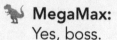 **MegaMax:**
Yes, boss.

 TrickiNiki has entered the castle

 FEARlix is freed

FEARlix:
Thanks, TrickiNiki!

 TrickiNiki has defeated the spider

AstroArchie:
Whoa! TrickiNiki's on fire!

FEARlix:
Keep it up!

TrickiNiki:
Ready team? You have to enter when
I say, and the castle is ours. I'm running
up the tower stairs.

AstroArchie:
Ready.

37

🦖 MegaMax:
Ready.

🐱 FEARlix:
Magic10 is coming after you TrickiNiki.
And there are spider eggs, which are
hatching and crawling all over the place!
I'll try to hold them off.

✏️ TrickiNiki:
Nearly there.

🐱 FEARlix:
Hurry!

✏️ TrickiNiki:
Archie and Max, use the catapult and fly
up here when I say. Getting close . . .
and . . . NOW!

 Team Jupiter has captured the castle!

🦖 MegaMax:
YESSSS!

🚀 AstroArchie:
Great work, TrickiNiki. And everyone.

FEARlix:
Those spiders were full on!

AstroArchie:
Niki, you there?

TrickiNiki:
Yeah, catch you later. Better get off before my imaginary bro catches me using his account. JOKING.

 TrickiNiki has left the game

Chapter 5

On the Monday morning, Niki and her friends were hanging outside, waiting for Ms Atlas to open their classroom.

'Don't move,' Eve said to Hamsa, calmly. She reached down and grabbed a stick.

'Why?' asked Hamsa.

'I'm just going to get this spider off your backpack.'

Hamsa squealed, throwing her backpack off and jumping around like her feet were on fire.

'I said don't move!' warned Eve, laughing.

'Is it gone? There's something in my hair!' Hamsa flung her head upside down and shook her hair like she was in a shampoo commercial. The others couldn't stop laughing. Eve took the backpack and flicked the spider off with the stick.

'Stay still, Ham,' said Eve, grabbing her shoulders and inspecting her hair. 'You're safe, there's nothing there.'

'Phew,' said Hamsa. 'And don't laugh at me – spiders are deadly.'

'Baby spiders are worse,' said Maggie. 'Imagine if a whole bunch hatched at once and came crawling after you.'

Hamsa shuddered at the thought and Niki noticed Maggie was looking at her with a cheeky smile.

'What do you think, Niki?' said Maggie. 'A whole bunch of baby spiders? How on earth would you defeat that?'

Niki looked at Maggie with her eyebrows raised. 'You're being weird, what's up?'

'Oh nothing,' said Maggie. 'Just adding a little *magic* to our Monday morning.'

Magic? thought Niki. She looked at Maggie as she pieced it together. 'Noooo! You're not . . .'

'I am.'

'Magic10!' said Niki. 'Magic Maggie more like it. You go, girl!' Niki gave her a high five.

'Ummm,' said Eve. 'What is going on?'

'Maggie showed up in the opposition team for Castle Capture yesterday. Correction. She didn't just "show up". She was SO good!'

Maggie blushed and Niki threw her arms around her friend.

'I've never seen you be so cheeky, Maggie, dropping hints like that. I love this side of you.'

Maggie couldn't stop smiling. 'I know, it's not the normal me, is it? But it was fun. My stepdad thinks the piano lessons are what makes me so speedy on the keyboard.'

'You should have seen my team's reaction. They were like "What the? Who's this new player?"' Niki thought back to the game. 'They totally thought you were a boy too. I can't wait to tell them after school!'

'Boys are so annoying,' said Hamsa.

Niki shook her head. 'Archie's cool. And his cousin Felix, who's on our team, he seems nice. It's just guys like Max who are painful.'

'They were pretty surprised at the LAN party to find out you were a girl. Have they said anything about it since?' asked Eve.

Niki thought back to Max's comments yesterday. Even though he'd been a jerk, she hadn't given it much thought since. 'That Max guy kept paying me out for being a girl.'

'You shouldn't put up with that,' said Hamsa.

Niki shrugged. 'It doesn't bother me, I got the last laugh by winning the game for us.'

'I don't know how you do it,' said Eve.

'Do what?'

'How you stay so positive and strong, even when people pick on you.'

'I need a lesson in how to do that,' admitted Hamsa.

'Me too,' said Maggie.

Niki tucked her hair behind her ears. 'I dunno. If people are rude or mean, you just ignore it.'

'It's not that simple,' said Eve.

'Why not?' said Niki. 'We're all in charge of our own feelings. Don't over think it. Don't over complicate it. Just get on with doing your own thing.'

'You should write a book,' said Hamsa. She moved her hands through the air like she was writing the title. 'Niki's Never-ending Words of Wisdom.'

'Oh, shut up,' said Niki, laughing.

'No, believe it or not, I'm giving you a compliment here,' said Hamsa.

'I'd buy your book,' said Maggie.

'I'd line up for an autographed copy,' added Eve.

'And I'd be your hustler,' said Hamsa, thinking back to the role she'd played in their Hackathon project. 'I'd book you for speaking gigs all over the world – we'd get to travel with you, of course. And I'd tell everyone that we knew you *before* you were famous!'

'All right, enough about the book,' said Niki. It felt good that her friends admired her so much, but they didn't need to bang on about it. She quickly thought of a way to change the subject. 'You know what, Maggie – you were good at CC. I'm going to ask my team if we can change to have five players.'

'But you said you've always liked playing in a four.'

'That was before Magic10 was on the scene!' said Niki, with a twinkle in her eye.

Maggie looked excited. 'I'd love that. And if anyone can convince them, it's you.'

Hamsa placed her hands in front of her chest, like she was pretending to hold a book. 'Niki's Never-ending Words of Wisdom: Chapter 256,' she said. 'How to stay confident and convince others.'

'Enough!' said Niki, playfully grabbing Hamsa in a bear hug and trying to cover her mouth. 'Chapter 257 . . . How to make your friends stop talking!'

Chapter
6

A few days later Niki invited Maggie over to her house after school. It was the first time they'd hung out, just them. And while they were an unlikely pair, it was fun that they now had something special in common.

Niki's bedroom walls were plastered with posters of iconic skaters, her shelves were stacked high with books and video-game cases and her wardrobe door was open, revealing the mess inside. But while her clothes were disorganised, the cabinet next to her desk was in pristine condition, displaying all her favourite shoes. She had classic sneakers, the best high-tops, and playful metallic boots.

Niki had her laptop on the desk with a keyboard and mouse connected. Her parents had a 'no computers in your room' rule, but they'd made an exception for Maggie's visit.

Maggie was sitting close by, eager to learn from the master. 'What was that move?' she asked, watching Niki glide her fingers across the keyboard.

'If you set up your key bindings right, you can combo your skills,' explained Niki, without taking her eyes off the screen. 'And depending on which character you're playing, it gives you a five-second boost of power.'

'Handy,' said Maggie, jotting down the instructions in her special journal. Niki glanced over and giggled.

'I love that you study so hard, even when the subject is video games,' said Niki.

Maggie laughed too. 'If I want to play in your team, I need to bring my A game.'

Maggie had already come a long way since the LAN party. Niki was itching for her to join the team, but at the same time, she didn't want to invite a total rookie in. It wouldn't be fair to Archie, Felix and Max.

Niki's mum came in with a basket of washing and plonked it on the bed for Niki to put away in her drawers.

'It's a beautiful day outside,' said her mum, in a tone that said: 'you should be out there instead of stuck in front of a screen.'

Niki had heard that one a thousand times before. 'Yep,' she said.

'Actually the forecast said it's going to turn ugly later. Maybe you girls could –'

'Yes, Mum. We'll finish this game and then I'll take Maggie home so we can get some "fresh air".'

'Okay,' said Mum. She lingered near the bed. 'You still playing Castle Capture?'

Niki rolled her eyes. It was one of those questions parents ask, even when they knew the answer.

'Yep.'

'And how are you coming along, Maggie?'

'Good thanks, Ms Apostolidis. Niki's a great teacher.'

'Is she?' said Mum, sounding surprised. 'Well, I could think of better ways to spend my time. Fifteen more minutes then outside.'

When her mum had left the room, Niki wriggled her shoulders like she was trying to untie stressful knots in her upper back. 'She. Does not. Get it.'

'I know,' said Maggie, checking over her shoulder to make sure Niki's mum had gone. 'And she makes it sound like you spend *all* your time glued to a screen. Surely you spend just as much time outside skateboarding as you do gaming.'

Niki nodded. 'Trouble is, my parents hate that I skate too. My older sister is the total opposite. I bet my parents wish I was more like her. But too bad, Mum and Dad – you're stuck with me.'

Niki typed a quick command and the sound of coins chinking came over the speakers. She'd just taken down the dragon.

'Nice one,' said Maggie, writing the move down. 'I guess I'm lucky. My parents don't mind me gaming, as long as we choose the games together. I think it's the fear of not knowing what I'm doing or who I'm playing with that scares them.'

'Exactly!' said Niki, feeling fired up. 'But Mum never asks me. She just assumes they're all pointless and make me anti-social. If she let me explain, it'd be so much easier.'

The laptop chimed with another alert.

'What was that sound?' asked Maggie, pen poised ready to take notes.

Niki laughed. 'Nothing for the game. Just a CC notification coming through.'

She opened up a window on the side of the screen to check it. Of course Niki was the type of multi-tasking boss who could read notifications *and* defend her place outside the castle's south wall at the same time.

Niki's hands were still typing at pace, but as she read the message, her typing slowed, until it came to a complete stop.

'No. Way,' she said slowly. 'No way! I'm in! I can't believe it, I'm actually in.'

Niki pushed out her seat and paced around the room.

'Into what?' asked Maggie.

'The esports team!' yelled Niki, her face beaming. She dived onto the bed and buried her head in the pillows to dampen her excited squeals.

'That's incredible!' said Maggie, sharing her excitement. She leant closer to the screen and scanned the message.

Congratulations

Niki Apostolidis

You have been selected from thousands of applications to compete in the first ever Junior Castle Capture Cup!

The event will take place at Centenary Stadium and be streamed live across the country.

Stay tuned for more details and, once again, well done!

Castle Capture Administration.

Maggie ran over to the bed and threw her arms around Niki. They were so excited they barely noticed Niki's eighteen-year-old sister, Eleni, arrive in the doorway.

'Did someone kill a cat in here?' said Eleni. Her hair was pulled back in a high bun and she was wearing lots of make-up.

'No,' said Niki, giving her sister a greasy.

'Well *someone* or *something* is making my eardrums bleed.'

'Sorry, Sis,' said Niki, forcing a big smile.

'Um, Niki,' said Maggie, who'd returned to the laptop. 'I think the team needs you. The opposition just released something called rainbow powder.'

'Oh, that's bad,' said Niki, bolting back. Eleni walked off muttering something about rainbows as Niki threw on her headset.

TrickiNiki:
We need to get together, fast! If you've got any reserves left in your bags, we can combine them and that SHOULD be enough to keep the rainbow powder from causing too much damage.

FEARlix:
I'm near the boathouse. Let's meet there.

MegaMax:
Done.

TrickiNiki:
On it.

AstroArchie:
On my way.

MegaMax:
Where did you go before, TrickiNiki? Thought we'd lost you.

TrickiNiki:
Sorry. Had to read something. Guess who'll be competing in the first ever Junior CC Cup!

AstroArchie:
What?

MegaMax:
You? You got on the team?

FEARlix:
When did they announce it?

TrickiNiki:
Just then, I'd registered to get notifications. You should check your CC profiles too.

MegaMax:
Are you joking, Nikoleta? It'll only be because the teams need equal boys and girls.

TrickiNiki:
I made the team because I'm good, Max.

MegaMax:
Yeah, right.

Maggie watched on as Niki opened her mouth, ready to fire an insult at Max. Then Niki paused, exhaled, and thought better of it. On screen the rainbow powder was all over the place, but she didn't care. Niki flicked the game off and slapped the laptop screen shut.

Maggie looked worried, like she was trying to work out what to say. 'I thought you said you never leave the game before it ends,' she said after a while.

Niki shrugged. 'Who cares. I just thought . . .' she stared at the laptop in front of them. 'I thought my team would be happy for me. Proud even. It's not like my family are going to be proud of me.'

Maggie put her hand on Niki's knee.

'I'd be excited if one of them made the team,' Niki went on. 'I should be celebrating right now, not justifying my place.'

'I know,' Maggie paused again as she thought. 'Maybe they feel threatened by how good you are. Or maybe they're disappointed that they didn't get in themselves.'

'But they haven't even checked their profiles yet. For all they know, they *are* in!'

Niki slumped back in her chair. She sighed. 'Whatever. I don't care what they think.' But as she stared out the window she was pretty sure Maggie could tell that she was lying. *What's wrong with me*, Niki thought. She was usually great at ignoring what other people thought or said about her. For some reason, this time it wasn't so easy.

'Mum was right. It's nice out,' said Niki after a while.

'Then we better get outside and enjoy it,' said Maggie, with a gentle smile.

Chapter
7

Maggie and Niki took the long way to Maggie's house, meandering through the park as Niki skated and Maggie rode alongside on her red, pink and orange bike. They didn't talk much, and that was exactly what Niki needed. She'd grown to love this about her friendship with Maggie. They were happy just to be in each other's company, without needing to fill the silence. And there was something so comforting about having someone nearby, even when you didn't feel like speaking.

'I wonder if the boys got in?' said Niki after a long time.

'I thought you didn't want to talk about it,' said Maggie.

'I don't . . . but I'm still curious,' Niki confessed as she leant into a turn on her board. 'I hope they did. Except for Max, maybe. He's never been a good teammate.'

'I must admit, he didn't make a great impression at the LAN party, or while I've watched you all play,' said Maggie. She pulled the cuffs of her school jumper up over her knuckles, to protect from the wind as she rode along. Their beautiful day was turning foul and heavy grey clouds were approaching. Within minutes the rain began.

'Come on! We'll get soaked if we're not home soon,' said Maggie, standing up from her seat to pedal faster.

'Won't we get more wet if we go fast?' asked Niki.

'How?'

'Because our bodies will be going *into* the rain as well as it hitting us on the head.'

'True,' said Maggie. 'But we'd also arrive quicker which means less time in the rain. There's got to be a formula for this.'

Niki enjoyed watching Maggie the Maths Magician try to figure it out in her head. When they arrived at Maggie's house they were drenched and no closer to an answer.

'Stay for a bit,' said Maggie, lifting her bike up the verandah stairs and leaning it against the wall. She took off her helmet and shook out her wet blonde hair.

'Thanks, but I'll head home,' said Niki hovering on the bottom step, just out of the rain.

'No way, it's pouring,' said Maggie.

Niki shrugged. 'I love the rain.'

'You can even stay for dinner if you like.'

'Thanks. I'm fine, honestly,' said Niki. The dinner offer did sound lovely, but with everything going on, Niki just wanted some space to reset and recharge.

Maggie groaned in frustration. 'Can you *for once* let someone help you?' she said.

Niki stepped out across the front yard. 'Nope. Besides you've got homework to do.'

'More CC study?' asked Maggie.

'No, silly,' said Niki with a smile. 'Working out our travelling-in-the-rain formula.'

And with that, Niki stepped on the end of her board, flipping up the other end and catching it. She walked out to the footpath, threw the board down in front of her then took a couple of steps to run and jump on.

Niki glided along, letting the rain soak in. She didn't care what her parents said about skateboarding. That it was rebellious, or punky, or a boy thing. There was nothing that made Niki feel more alive, or more at peace, than being out on her board. And skating in the rain was the most peaceful thing of all.

She loved the feeling of it hitting her face, the fresh smell and how the sound made her feel like she could block out the whole world.

She went home the same way through the park, carefully avoiding the puddles. She breathed in the fresh air but when she exhaled her shoulders still felt tense. Niki's mind kept going back to her gaming friends and how they treated her differently now they knew she was a girl. Max was stupid, but she weirdly felt uncomfortable with Archie too. It was kind of him to stick up for her, but she didn't want to be rescued. She was used to looking after herself and this kind of self-doubt put her on unfamiliar ground. Her friends always said she was strong and independent, so why was Niki letting these boys get into her head.

Distracted, Niki rode through a puddle,

the water sprayed up either side of the board, drenching her shoes.

'Snap out of it,' she said to herself angrily, but her mind felt like it had a mind of its own.

She turned the corner into her street and was on the home straight. That's when it happened.

Niki clipped the edge of the pavement and went flying off her board. She lay on the footpath. Alone. In the rain. And broken.

Chapter 8

Niki sat on the hospital bed while the doctor stuck X-rays onto a light box on the wall. Her wrists were grazed and still stinging. It was a few hours since her fall, but as she sat with her mum and dad, Niki braced herself and hoped for good news.

'It's a nasty one,' said the doctor, examining the X-rays and writing patient notes on her clipboard. 'Your right hand is heavily bruised but not broken. On the left side though, you've fractured the scaphoid bone. It's part of a group of bones in your wrist called your metacarpus. And, see here,' she pointed to the X-ray, 'the scaphoid is just at the bottom of your thumb.'

'Ouch,' said Dad.

'What does that mean though?' asked Niki. 'How long am I out for?'

'Out for?' asked the doctor, almost laughing. 'You sound like a footy player.'

'Close enough,' said Niki, thinking about the tournament. 'How long?'

The doctor took another look at the X-ray then sat down in front of Niki and her parents. 'The fracture is what we call "non-displaced", so the good news is that you don't need to have surgery.'

Niki held her breath. *Was there bad news?*

'In fact,' the doctor continued. 'You only need a cast for six weeks. You'll be able to –'

'Six weeks!' yelled Niki. 'No way, that's too long.'

'I'm afraid that's how long an injury like this takes to heal,' said the doctor.

'And it sounds like we're lucky things weren't worse,' her dad added. 'Imagine if you didn't have your helmet on? Or if you'd landed on the road and then –'

'Stop, I can't think about all the what ifs,' said Niki's mum, covering her ears. 'Niki, I know you're disappointed, but it's just a video game, darling.'

'Mum,' Niki groaned. 'It's more than just a game to me. There's never been a big tournament like this before and missing out is *not* an option. There has to be another way.' Niki pulled herself together and looked at the doctor. 'I have a mega important competition in one month and I can't compete without my hands. If I have to do ten hours of rehab a day, I promise I'll do it. I'll do anything.'

The doctor sighed and looked at Niki thoughtfully. 'I'm so sorry, Nikoleta, but all the rehab in the world won't make your bones heal that fast. And if you rush these things, you risk adding time to your recovery, or maybe needing surgery after all. C'mon, let's go see the nurse and we'll have your cast put on.'

The doctor led them out to the foyer where they took a seat and waited for the nurse. Niki's mind was a blur. She'd torn a hole in her favourite jeans, she'd lost any chance of her parents letting her skate to Maggie's house unsupervised but, above all else, she was heartbroken about the competition. Her whole body ached, and it wasn't that the painkillers were starting to wear off. It was the brutal mix of disappointment, sadness and anger.

When Dad went to fill in the paperwork at the counter, Mum put her arm around Niki. She brushed it off coldly. 'Oh, sweetheart,' said Mum. 'I'm so sorry.'

'Whatever,' Niki said under her breath. She looked down at her hands, imagining she was at the keyboard. She tried wriggling her fingers, practising some of the CC sequences, but it was impossible. To move her fingers, even just a little, was excruciating. A tear rolled down her cheek.

'You don't get it,' said Niki. 'You have no idea what this means to me.'

'I know I don't get it,' said Mum. 'But I love you. And I'm here for you no matter what.'

While Niki worked hard to hold in the tears, Mum tried to put her arm around her again. And this time, Niki didn't brush it away.

Chapter 9

Niki had the next day off school, with her mum insisting she needed to rest. Then the following morning, Mum walked Niki all the way into school.

'I can manage by myself, you know,' said Niki.

'I'm sure you can,' said Mum with a smile. 'I just want to chat to Ms Atlas and work out if there's any way to make the next six weeks more comfortable for you.'

'I'm getting out of this thing in less than

six weeks, remember,' said Niki, holding up her arm with the cast.

'If you say so,' said Mum, gently.

Niki didn't care what her parents or the doctor said. She wasn't ready to give up her place in the team.

As they approached the classroom Niki braced herself. She didn't feel strong, but if she was going to get through this, she needed to find courage from somewhere. That strength was a bit like choosing the right character for a game. She needed to play the confident, indestructible old Niki, even though reality felt very different.

'Niki! What happened?' screamed Hamsa, rushing across the room when Niki entered. Eve and Maggie were close behind.

'Are you okay?' asked Eve. 'We thought it was weird you weren't at school yesterday.'

'And even weirder when you didn't reply to any messages last night,' added Hamsa.

'It was the rain, wasn't it?' said Maggie. 'Did you have an accident going home the other night?'

'Yeah, it's not bad though,' said Niki, finally getting a word in.

Maggie shook her head in frustration. 'I told you to stay at my house. Why didn't you listen?'

'It wasn't the rain's fault,' said Niki.

'Then whose fault was it?' asked Hamsa, looking worried. 'Were you hit by a car? Or struck by lightning in that storm?'

'No,' said Niki, laughing. She could always rely on Hamsa to bring the drama. Deep down Niki knew being distracted was what caused the accident, but she wasn't ready to admit that. 'It was just one of those freak things,' she managed.

While her Mum chatted with Ms Atlas at the front of the room, Niki had attracted quite the audience, with most of her class huddled around her to hear the story. Unlike Hamsa, Niki did not like the attention.

'Niki, did you hear the bones snap?' asked Katherine.

'Was there lots of blood?' asked Ezra.

'Can we sign your cast?' asked Ayla, with her favourite red marker in hand.

'No, no and not sure,' answered Niki. 'It's so not a big deal.'

She moved her way through the crowd of kids and sat down at their regular table. Her friends joined her and Hamsa enjoyed acting like Niki's bodyguard, instructing her classmates to give them space.

'I can't believe you didn't tell us,' said Eve.

'I know,' Hamsa added. 'I would have been all like "ahhh, everyone, I need lots of sympathy!"'

'It's funny because it's true,' said Eve, winking at Hamsa.

'Not our Niki though,' said Hamsa, putting her arm around her. 'She's as tough as they come.'

Niki forced a smile, feeling anything but tough.

'You're left-handed too,' said Eve. 'How are you going to write?'

'And what does this mean for the big CC tournament?' asked Maggie.

'Oh yeah,' said Hamsa. 'Maggie told us yesterday you got into the team. This is mega news. And we're totally coming along as your cheer squad.'

Niki couldn't look at them. She shrugged. 'The doctor said recovery takes six weeks.'

Maggie gasped. 'Oh Niki, you'll miss the comp. This is all my fault.'

'It is not,' said Niki, firmly. 'It was my choice to skate home. I can only blame myself.'

'Have you told the CC guys about the accident?' asked Maggie. 'Do you even know if they made the esports team too?'

'They did,' said Niki. She'd looked it up yesterday and, sure enough, all four of them were in a team together. 'I haven't told them about the accident because, as far as I'm concerned, I'm not missing the comp. I just have to prove the doctor wrong and get better sooner,' she said, trying her best to sound positive.

'Well, anything we can do to help, you just name it,' said Eve.

Niki nodded. And as the morning went by, she realised her friends really did mean '*anything*'. Eve, who had the best handwriting, wrote down all of Niki's answers for their history quiz, while Maggie and Hamsa made sure she didn't have to lift a finger.

When Ms Atlas instructed them to get their maths books, Niki went to stand.

'No way, Ni-kay,' said Hamsa, ushering her to sit down again.

'You know I'm not completely useless,' said Niki. 'I can carry a book.'

'But we want to help,' said Maggie.

'The best way to help right now, is to pretend it's not happening,' said Niki.

'Okay,' said Maggie, reluctantly.

Niki went to collect their books, she struggled as she pulled them from the shelf, and accidentally knocked others out. She took it in her stride, balancing the books in her arms as she walked back. It wasn't just awkward, it was painful too, as her wrist without the cast still ached from the bruises.

When lunchtime rolled around, Niki was determined to look after herself. She managed to unwrap her sandwich without too much trouble, and pretended she didn't want her biscuits so she didn't have to admit she couldn't open the packet. When it came to her drink bottle, Niki was stuck. She tried lodging the bottle between her left arm and her body, while unscrewing the lid with her right hand, but it wouldn't budge. Niki saw Eve and Hamsa sharing a concerned look. 'I can do this,' she snapped, before they had the chance to offer help.

While Niki continued to struggle, she noticed her friends were trying to avoid looking at her, like they didn't want Niki to feel she was in the spotlight. Frustrated, Niki put the bottle back down on the table. 'Whatever, I'm not thirsty anyway,' she said. But how long would she be able to keep this up?

Chapter 10

There is a saying that 'time heals all wounds', but for Niki things only got worse. A week had passed and she still found it a daily struggle to accept help from others.

'I can do that for you,' said Eleni when she walked into the living room.

Niki was sitting cross-legged on the couch with her skateboard in her lap. She'd busted the back of it in the accident and was trying to tighten the trucks. She looked at her sister. 'You? Fix a skateboard? As if you know how to do that.'

'I don't,' admitted Eleni. 'But you can teach me. I'll be more useful than you right now.'

Niki inspected her work. Her sister was right. She'd been trying for twenty minutes and had got nowhere. 'Fine. Take this,' she said, handing Eleni the spanner.

Eleni sat next to Niki and took the tool and board. Niki found it so funny seeing her gorgeous sister with perfectly manicured nails holding a skateboard.

'If I break a nail doing this, you're in big trouble,' said Eleni, smiling.

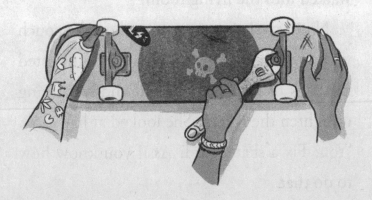

'Fair enough,' said Niki.

She showed Eleni what was needed.

'I can't believe you want to get back on this thing,' said Eleni. 'Aren't you scared you'll have another accident?'

Niki shrugged. 'Not enough to stop me. I miss it so bad. It's my exercise, my adventure and my relaxation all in one. I feel like part of me is missing without it. Maybe it's how you'd feel if you didn't have your nails done.'

Eleni shuddered at the thought. 'I feel naked and gross when that happens.'

Niki rolled her eyes. 'That's so lame,' she teased.

They'd made some progress with the board when Niki's dad came in.

'What are you up to?' he asked as he pulled some vegies out of the fridge to start dinner.

'I'm *finally* getting around to fixing my board,' said Niki.

'And I'm helping,' said Eleni, proudly. 'I bet you never thought you'd see me holding a . . . what's this thing called?'

'A spanner,' said Dad, laughing. 'And yes, that's a first.' He paused a moment before adding. 'You know you can't ride that thing, Niki.'

She hated how her family called her favourite possession 'that thing'.

'Because of my wrist?' she asked.

'Yes, because of your wrist. And the grazes. And because you ended up in hospital and gave your mother and me heart attacks.'

Niki felt annoyed. Although she had to admit, it was fair enough he didn't want her riding with a broken wrist. 'Fine,' she said after a while. 'I'll get it ready for when I'm out of my cast.'

'No,' said Dad, as he continued to cut the carrots. 'I mean you can't ride it ever.'

'What?' said Niki, angrily.

'Mum and I discussed it and it's not safe. A young girl like you shouldn't be out on the streets riding a thing like that.'

'Stop calling it a "thing"!'

'A skateboard then,' said Dad, keeping his cool.

'So, what, a bike would be okay? Or a scooter? But not my board.'

'Well . . .'

'How will I get to school?'

'You can walk,' said Dad.

'That is so unfair!' said Niki. 'You can't take this away from me. Please, Dad. You can't!'

Dad put the carrots down and looked at Niki. 'The decision's final, Niki. No more skateboarding.'

‧ ‧ ‧

At school Niki found each day more and more frustrating, but her friends hadn't given up on her.

'Check these out,' said Hamsa, showing Niki her tablet. They were sitting in class before recess and Hamsa had a browser open with loads of tabs for different websites.

Niki leant over to take a look. Her arm was outstretched while Eve carefully drew on her cast.

'So gaming is your "thang",' said Hamsa. 'And you obviously can't play that CC one right now, BUT there are other games that you don't even need your hands for. I did some research and these look fun.'

Hamsa talked the girls through the games she'd found. There was a pig counting game operated by voice controls, and an epic fantasy that used brand-new controllers specially designed for accessibility. There was even a headset you could wear that allowed you to swim through the ocean with elephant seals.

'Thanks,' said Niki in a flat voice. 'I'm not into pigs and that controller and VR stuff is expensive.'

'I know,' said Hamsa. 'You wouldn't be able to buy it all, but maybe you could borrow them. It gives us something to think about, anyway.'

Niki was tired of the conversation, and she'd forgotten Eve was in the middle of her artwork. She shifted in her chair and Eve's marker slipped down the cast, drawing a big line through her drawing.

'Niki!' groaned Eve. 'You've ruined it.'

'Sorry,' said Niki. She folded her arms in front of herself. 'You know the cast looks fine as it is. Thanks anyway.'

Eve looked disappointed as she returned her markers to her pencil case.

Maggie eventually broke the silence. 'The Team Jupiter crew have been asking why you're not on CC. But don't worry, I've been thinking up creative excuses for you. And they've bought them every time.'

'Ta,' said Niki, without looking up. She hated that she needed everyone's help all the time.

'Oh and I've worked out the formula for you,' added Maggie. Niki looked confused, and Maggie took out her book to show her. 'My stepdad and I did some research about whether you get less wet if you run in the rain instead of walk. Turns out I was right, according to this formula at least. Running instead of walking, or in our case, riding our bikes and boards faster, is the best way to stay dry.'

Niki didn't even look at Maggie's book. She looked down at her wrist and when the bell rang for recess, Hamsa and Maggie stood up quickly.

'I'll take that for you,' said Hamsa, reaching for Niki's pencil case.

'Leave it!' barked Niki. The girls stopped in shock. And Niki felt awful. 'Sorry. I didn't mean for it to come out like that. I know you're all trying to help, but honestly, I don't need you.'

And with that, Niki pushed back her chair and stormed out of the room. When the girls looked around they realised the whole class was watching.

'Skater Girl's mad,' said their classmate, Michelle, in a sing song voice.

'Excuse me,' warned Ms Atlas, looking at Michelle with her eyebrows raised. 'You heard the bell, everyone. Outside, now.'

The rest of the students headed for the door and Ms Atlas came over. 'Everything okay, girls?' she asked gently.

Hamsa nodded. 'Niki's just angry about her hand. I don't blame her. I got a mozzie bite on one of my knuckles last year. SO annoying. It ruined the whole month.'

Maggie couldn't help but laugh.

'I'm serious!' said Hamsa. 'Do you know how hard it is to scratch your knuckles!'

'No, but it sounds dreadful,' said Ms Atlas as she walked away.

Maggie and Hamsa collected their things, but Eve was slower to move. 'I can't believe Niki!' she said. 'We have been doing everything we can to help her, and she's so ungrateful.'

'I guess she has been a little rude,' said Maggie.

'A little?' said Eve, rolling her eyes.

'Give her a break,' said Hamsa.

Eve stood back and looked at Hamsa like she was a stranger. 'Really? That's funny coming from you. You never stick up for Niki.'

'I know. But she's our friend. And she needs us whether she likes it or not.'

'I get it now,' said Eve, nodding. 'You *like* helping her because it annoys her.'

'Annoying Niki is in my top five hobbies,' said Hamsa with a wink. 'But seriously, we need to step up and take action here. Niki hasn't been herself since the accident, and she needs us. Who's with me?'

Chapter 11

'One for Hamsa, one for Eve, one for me, and ...' Maggie took the fourth baseball cap out of her schoolbag. It was the next morning at school and the girls were catching up before they tracked down Niki.

Eve and Hamsa squealed when they saw what Maggie had made. It was a black baseball cap with bright orange felt letters that said COACH across the top.

'You're the best, Maggie,' said Eve, wrapping her in a hug. 'How on earth did you make it so quickly?'

'*And* make it so good?' added Hamsa.

Maggie blushed. 'Eve found an online program to design the font and the letters. Then she showed me the pattern, I printed it out, transferred it to the felt, and used my glue gun to stick it on. I can make us extra-blingy hats for game day if we like.'

'Oh yes, we like!' said Hamsa, rubbing her hands together. 'But first, we need to recruit our coach.'

They did a lap around the school, checking all the usual places where Niki might be, and found her sitting on a bench outside the library.

When Niki saw them coming, her tummy felt wobbly. She knew she would have hurt their feelings yesterday, but she didn't know how to apologise.

'It's not open,' she said, nodding her head towards the library door.

'That's okay,' said Maggie.

She sat down next to Niki while Eve and Hamsa stood opposite them. Niki noticed they were all wearing hats.

'Did someone forget to tell me it was "wear your black hat day"?' said Niki.

'We didn't forget,' said Maggie. She smiled and pulled the coach's hat out of her schoolbag. She handed it to Niki.

Niki studied the hat, feeling a bit confused. 'What exactly am I coaching?' she asked.

'We've got a proposal,' Hamsa butted in. 'It must be mega upsetting to miss the CC tournament.'

Maggie agreed. 'You're a great player and we know how important it is to you.'

'If we could turn back time, we would,' said Eve.

'But we can't,' said Hamsa, trying to stay upbeat. 'We need to cop it on the chin and get on with life. Just like you would have written about in *Niki's Never-ending Words of Wisdom*, Chapter 842 – How to turn that frown upside-down.'

Niki ran the hat through her fingers. Despite Hamsa's efforts, she didn't find the joke funny. 'How am I supposed to do that?' she asked.

'By agreeing to coach our team,' said Hamsa.

'*Our* team?' Niki quizzed, wondering how her three friends, who'd never heard of Castle Capture three weeks ago, were suddenly competing in a national competition.

'Yes,' Hamsa said. 'You said yourself that Maggie's a natural. We propose she takes your place on the team, playing alongside Max, Archie and Felix. Eve and I will head up the cheer squad, and you, Niki Apostolidis, will be our fearless leader.'

'I still have a lot to learn,' said Maggie. 'But with you as my coach, I think we can do it.'

'Not just *do it*,' said Eve. 'We can win this thing!'

As Hamsa prepared the cheer squad's victory dance, Eve couldn't help but be swept up in the fun. Niki wasn't so sure though.

'What's up?' Maggie asked her gently.

Niki shrugged. She'd been such a bad friend, she didn't deserve to have the girls rallying around her. 'It won't work, anyway,' she said. 'The tournament organisers won't let one player replace another.'

'I've checked and they will,' said Maggie. 'I'll be nervous as anything, but I really believe that together, you and I can do this. What have you got to lose?'

Nothing, thought Niki, although something was still holding her back. She looked over to see Hamsa practising a handstand with Eve trying to help hold her legs in the air. As Hamsa yelled instructions to Eve, Niki shook her head and laughed. 'They are such dorks.'

'Yep,' said Maggie. 'But they're *our* dorks.'

Niki nodded and looked down at her hat again. 'Coach, hey?' She tried the hat on for size. 'Does the coach get to approve the cheer squad dances?' Niki asked with her eyebrows raised cheekily.

'Of course,' said Maggie.

'Then I'm in.'

Niki clutched her training notes folder under her arm and walked with her friends towards the LAN café. It was the weekend and their first official training session. Niki's mum, Angela, and Maggie's dad, Paul, had come along too.

'Doesn't one of the boys in your team live interstate?' asked Angela.

'Yep,' said Maggie. 'Felix will jump online from where he lives and join us that way. Even though he's not here, it's best for the rest of us to train in person.'

'Why?' asked Angela. 'If you play online, can't you train online too? It would've saved us all the trip out here.'

'I'm all for virtual reality,' said Niki. 'But some things work better in *real* reality.'

'Like eating ice creams,' said Eve, licking her lips. 'Not that I've tried it in VR, but give me real ice cream any day.'

'Me too,' said Paul. He had the same white-blond hair as Maggie and the same gentle, happy eyes. 'I'm pumped for today – to see how on earth you train for an electronic sport. Is it like normal sport, where you do a warm-up, some drills, a practice match and talk strategy?'

'Our legendary coach will be able to answer that soon,' said Maggie, excitedly.

Niki swallowed hard. It was great that her friends had so much faith in her. She just hoped she was up for the challenge.

When they walked inside the café Yumi greeted them from across the room. She was wearing a white t-shirt, tartan skirt and silver trainers.

'Hello, girls, *chickas*, *on'nanoko*!' she said, hurrying over. 'Niki, I love your cast.'

Niki held up her wrist so Yumi could take a closer look. 'Eve did all the drawings. Pretty cool, huh.'

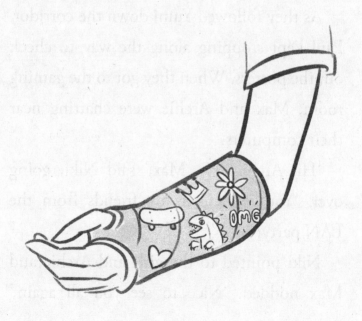

Yumi nodded and smiled at Eve.

'It's still not finished,' explained Eve.

'Ignore her,' Niki told Yumi as she gave Eve a playful nudge. 'She is the world's biggest perfectionist.'

'Well, it looks perfect to me,' said Yumi. 'Come on through. Archie and Max are here already and I've put a whole section aside out back so you won't be interrupted.'

As they followed Yumi down the corridor, Paul kept stopping along the way to check out the posters. When they got to the gaming room, Max and Archie were chatting near their computers.

'Hi, Archie. Hi, Max,' said Niki, going over. 'You remember my friends from the LAN party?'

Niki pointed to the girls and Archie and Max nodded. 'Nice to see you all again,' said Archie. 'And to meet you, Magic10, in person . . . now that I know who you really are. You know, I've tried so many times to enter the castle the way you did in that first match. I still haven't nailed it.'

'Oh, thanks,' said Maggie. 'I'll teach you some time.'

'How're your hands going?' Max asked Niki.

'They're rubbish. But whatever,' Niki said. 'Should we get down to business?'

Maggie, Niki and the boys sat next to each other at the computers. They put their headsets on and greeted Felix, who'd just joined them online. Paul and Angela sat down to observe from the other side of the room, while Hamsa and Eve were at the next table along, supposedly planning their outfits for the big day, but pretty much just listening in.

When they were all settled, Niki kneeled high on her chair so she could see everyone's faces.

'So, hi. This is weird,' she began. 'But because I can't use my stupid hand, I'm the lucky gal who'll be your coach. Annoying for me that I don't get to play, but super exciting for Maggie. And I know she'll smash it.'

'Welcome to the team, Maggie,' said Felix through the headset.

'Thanks, I won't let you down,' said Maggie.

Niki continued. 'I'm not here to boss you around, or tell you stuff you already know. But I *am* here to make sure we win. I know we can do it. We just need to communicate well, train hard and have the right strategy.'

Max, Archie and Maggie were smiling and nodding. Niki felt a real buzz in the air. 'All right, let's warm up with a game. One

106

twist – you have to play as a character you've never played before.'

'What!' Archie complained. 'I love being Elvon and Elf.'

'And no one plays Brutus as good as me,' added Max.

'I know,' said Niki. 'We all have our favourites, but we need to understand *every* character in the game. That way, when the opposition choose them, we'll already know their strengths and weaknesses. Plus, we'll be able to play them ourselves if our favourite characters get banned.'

'Excuse me,' said Paul, putting his hand up to get Niki's attention. 'What do you mean by "banning characters"?'

'It's how a tournament starts,' replied Niki. 'There's a draft and each team takes it in turns to pick and ban characters.'

'A draft?' asked Angela as she scrolled through her phone, seemingly disinterested.

'Just wait until game day,' said Max. 'You'll love it!'

'For example,' explained Archie, 'your opposition might pick Scarlet, who's this awesome sorcerer. So when it's *your* turn, you'd probably pick Corse.'

'Corse is half-cat, half-horse,' added Maggie. 'He has the power to reverse spells, so it's a good match against Scarlet.'

'Gotcha,' said Paul.

'There's another option,' said Niki.

'Of course there is,' said Hamsa, in support.

'You could *ban* instead of *pick*,' said Niki. 'You see, there's a character called Multiply. He's human, but can use his eyebrows to multiply everything. So when he's on the same team as Scarlet it's mega dangerous.'

'If Multiply is so good, why doesn't everyone automatically choose him first,' asked Eve.

'Because Multiply is really rubbish at defending himself,' said Niki. 'Every character has strengths and weaknesses. Just like us humans do.'

'Wow,' said Paul, scratching his head. 'This is more involved than I realised.'

Angela laughed. 'I'll order us some coffees. It might be a long afternoon.'

'By "long" I think you mean "fun", Mum,' said Niki, wishing that for once her mum didn't put down the game she loved so much.

During the warm up Niki studied the characters, as well as the players themselves, writing notes messily as they played.

'Well done,' she said when they'd finished. 'Maggie, there's a key binding that lets you position the rainbow *and* defend the pot of gold at the same time, I'll show you after. And I'm going to make a character handbook so we can get the best strategy for the draft.'

'I'll help you type it out,' offered Eve.

Niki looked down at her hand, frustrated that she wouldn't be able to make the book herself. She reluctantly accepted. 'Thanks, Eve. I'll chuck it online too so we can all view and add to it.'

'Then, after the tournament, we could re-brand the handbook and sell it to other players,' said Hamsa, seeming proud that she was able to contribute.

Niki smiled, thinking back to the Hackathon. 'We're not selling all our hard work, Hamsa. Although, I do love seeing you hustle.'

'I love to use my hustle muscles,' said Hamsa with a wink.

As training rolled on, Niki felt more and more comfortable calling the shots. And it felt like the team were getting a lot out of it, even Max who was quieter than he normally was when playing online. They had a break halfway through and had milkshakes out in the cafe and Yumi checked in on their progress.

'It's going great, I think,' said Niki.

'I so hope your team take out the title,' said Yumi.

'We can make you an outfit if you want to join the cheer squad,' offered Hamsa.

'Oh that's so kind,' said Yumi. 'But I'm working at the tournament, so I better not play favourites.'

After the break, Team Jupiter were just as productive and Niki couldn't believe how quickly time flew.

'That'll do for today,' she said, when it was time to go. 'We've got a few more online training sessions after school, one more meet up, and then we're on. We can do this.'

'Goooooooo team!' called Eve and Hamsa, rolling their hands up into the air and ending with a star jump.

Everyone laughed.

'That's not one of our main moves,' Hamsa was quick to explain. 'We're still working on the full routine!'

'You and Eve will be great. We all will be. Until next time, team!'

'Till next time,' said Felix through the headsets.

'Thanks, Niki,' said Archie.

'Yeah, thanks,' said Max, without looking Niki in the eye.

'Oh I nearly forgot,' said Niki. 'I have some homework for you.'

'What?' protested Max.

'Not for you,' said Niki. 'Archie, Maggie and Felix, I'll send you some stuff to work on before our next training. No pressure, but you can do it if you like.'

'Definitely,' said Maggie.

'Anything to help,' Archie added.

They packed up their things, said goodbye to Yumi and the girls made their way back to the cars.

'Pssst,' said Hamsa. 'I'm not doubting your coaching skills, but why'd you give the others homework and not Max?'

'Because I'm pretty sure they're the type of people who like to be given a task, then tick it off.'

'Yep, you know me well,' said Maggie, slinging her crocheted bag over her shoulder.

'Max, on the other hand, is the type who'd want to work it out for himself,' Niki continued. 'It's his ego. I know that in the end he'll train as hard as the others – otherwise he'll be scared they might look better than him on game day.'

'Got it. Gee you're smart,' said Hamsa.

'She's right,' added Paul who was walking alongside Angela. 'Working out how people learn and their different motivations is half the battle. You're a natural coach, Niki.'

'Hmmm.' Angela nodded with a smile. Niki thought that might have been her mum's attempt at being proud of her, although it was never that easy to tell with Mum.

When they jumped in the car Niki was already planning the next training in her head. They had four sessions to go. She just hoped it would be enough for their team to win.

Chapter 13

'Can I play with you?' Eleni asked Niki. It was nearly bedtime and Niki was sitting with her sister on the couch. Her tablet was nestled in her lap.

Niki raised her eyebrows and looked at her sister. 'For reals?' she asked. 'You've *never* asked to game with me.'

'Well, you've never invited me,' said Eleni, before adding. 'I also kind of like the colours and music on this game.'

She was right there. Niki was playing a simple 'match 3' game, something she could play despite her broken wrist. It was one of the many games Hamsa had recommended after the accident.

Niki moved the tablet so it was sitting between her and Eleni. 'Aim is to pair the cats with their kittens as quick as possible.'

'Sounds easy,' said Eleni.

Niki rolled her eyes at her big sister's confidence. 'All right, Katherine Johnson, good luck.'

'Who's Katherine Johnson?' asked Eleni.

'This brainiac NASA maths chick. Clearly you must be smarter than her if this game is "easy".'

Eleni poked her tongue out at Niki and took up the challenge. It was easy at first. As the different coloured cats poked their heads in and out around the screen, Eleni was able to remember where their partner was and tap the screen to pair them up.

After a while, it wasn't so easy.

Beep! The music changed and 'GAME OVER' flashed across the screen.

'Awww, not fair,' said Eleni. 'Give me another go.'

Niki happily obliged. It was the first time Eleni had shown an interest in gaming. And it was fun to do it together. This time she bowed out at the same place.

'Where are you, stupid kitty?' said Eleni, playfully.

'Behind the fridge,' said Niki pointing to the screen.

'Ohhh,' said Eleni. 'Let's play together this time then.'

Niki hit the 'NEW GAME' button and the sisters huddled in closely, helping each other out as they sped through the first round.

'Gotcha!' called Eleni as she tapped on the fridge, pairing the purple tabby kitten with its mum.

'Nice,' said Niki. 'Now, you watch the top half of the screen and I'll take the bottom, that way none of these sneaky cats will get past us.'

They worked together, beating their top-score each time before making a mistake and heading back to the start. It was easier now they'd remembered the exact pattern from before.

'You excited about Saturday?' asked Eleni, going through the motions on those easy first levels.

Niki nodded. 'Still wish I was in the team, though.'

'Yeah, that sucks,' said Eleni. 'You're lucky your friends have been so supportive.'

Niki groaned, louder than she meant to. 'Sorry, that sounded ungrateful,' she said quickly. 'My friends have been awesome. I'm so lucky to have them. But I just . . .' Niki stopped. It felt weird talking about her feelings, and to her sister of all people. At least it was easier with a screen between them, and not having to look each other in the eye.

'It's nothing,' Niki said finally. 'Guess I'm just peeved Mum and Dad are threatening to never let me skate again.'

'They'll come around, don't worry.' Eleni reassured her. 'When I was your age they were furious because they thought I wasted all my time on make-up and clothes.'

'Really?' said Niki, looking up at Eleni. 'I mean, I can imagine the make-up part, but not them being angry at you. I thought you were the prefect daughter and I was the troublemaker.'

'As if! You would not believe the fights we used to have,' said Eleni. 'One time, Mum confiscated all my nail polishes and I slammed my bedroom door so hard the doorknob broke off.'

'Whoa! It's like neither of us fit their expectations, but for opposite reasons.'

'Exactly,' said Eleni, as she paired the green cats without missing a beat of the game. 'Please don't let it get you down. Even though our parents don't always understand the things we love, it doesn't mean they don't love us. They just have an annoying way of showing it, that's all.

Niki scoffed. Annoying seemed like an understatement.

'You've got to be you though, Niki,' said Eleni. 'As long as "being you" doesn't hurt other people, you should go right on doing it.'

'That's the trouble,' said Niki, now feeling more relaxed around her sister. 'I don't really . . . I don't even know what 'me' is anymore.'

'Why?' asked Eleni.

Niki shrugged. 'My friends are always like: "Oh Niki, you're so independent. You're so strong, you're so confident". I don't feel like me because I'm none of those things right now. I can't do up my shoelaces. I need help carrying my books. And, for a while there, I let some stupid boy on an ego trip get into my head and make me doubt myself. It's like I'm the total opposite of confident.'

Eleni gently placed her hand on Niki's shoulder. 'You do know, right, part of being confident is being able to admit when you need help? Letting other people help you doesn't make you weak. It makes you even stronger.'

'Since when have you been so wise?' said Niki.

'Since forever,' joked Eleni. 'Seriously, though, your bones will get better soon. It's more important that you don't let anyone break this.' She gently tapped Niki on the head.

Niki looked up from the screen, grateful for her sister's support. She managed a smile, before they heard the familiar game-over music.

'That was your fault,' said Niki, resetting the game.

'Yeah right,' said Eleni.

They worked through the game again, beating their top score. And Niki wondered whether her sister was right. Maybe she was as strong as she'd always been? Maybe figuring that out made her even stronger.

Chapter 14

'Oh. My. Goodness,' said Maggie, standing with her dad, Paul, Niki and Niki's mum out the front of Centenary Stadium. It was normally home to basketball, tennis and netball matches, but today a different sport was in town.

They were a hundred meters from the stadium, and the entire space was packed. As they weaved their way through the crowds, they passed booths set up by game developers showcasing their new releases. There were food trucks too with smells of rich curries, cinnamon jam doughnuts and salty hot chips filling the air.

'I know what I'm having for lunch,' said Paul, eyeing off the burger truck. 'I can't believe how many people are here. And it's not even game time.'

'Look! It's Scarlet the Sorcerer!' cried Maggie, pointing to a woman dressed head to toe in the red snake-like scales that the Scarlet character was famous for.

'Cosplay is so ridiculously cool,' said Niki.

'Cosplay?' asked Niki's mum, who was unfamiliar with the term.

'It stands for costume play,' Niki explained. 'It's when you dress up as a character from something like a comic, anime, movie or video game. The fans get right into it at tournaments and conventions.'

'Wow! It makes the games so *real*,' said Maggie with a twinkle in her eye. It was like she was already designing a costume in her head.

'Are we allowed to come in and out of the stadium?' asked Maggie. 'There's too much to take in here and I don't want to miss it!'

'Yep, our tickets let us go anywhere,' said Niki. 'So we can do some exploring and get some fresh air later. But first . . .'

Niki pointed to the stadium entrance – itching to get started. She and Maggie had arrived early for registration and the cheer squad were meeting them later.

Inside the stadium there was a wide corridor that ran all the way around. It was busy there too, with merchandise stands, food and drink areas and people queuing up for the toilets already. Niki followed the signs to the registration desk. Max, Felix and Archie, along with their parents, were waiting for them. Max and Archie looked more dressed up than they did at the LAN café, with fresh haircuts too. And Felix looked how Niki had imagined – an older-looking, less space-obsessed version of Archie.

'Finally!' said Niki, throwing her hands in the air excitedly. 'All the members of Team Jupiter in the same state! Felix, it's awesome to meet you in person.'

'Sure is,' he said, shaking hands with her and Maggie before giving Archie a hearty slap on the back.

They signed in at the desk and the whole team were issued with Access All Areas passes to wear around their necks. Paul and Angela received them too, given that they'd been chosen to be the adult chaperones.

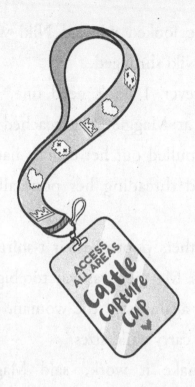

'And here are your uniforms,' said the woman behind the registration desk. She handed orange and black t-shirts to Max, Archie, Maggie and Felix.

'Um, excuse me, our coach needs a shirt too,' said Maggie, pointing at Niki.

'Sorry, kiddo, it's only for competitors.'

Maggie looked worried Niki would feel left out. Niki shrugged.

'Whatever. I don't need one,' she said, winking at Maggie. She reached into her bag and pulled out her coach's hat, putting it on and threading her ponytail through the back.

The others popped their t-shirts on over their tops. Maggie's was way too big.

'Sorry again,' said the woman. 'We don't normally carry child sizes.'

'I'll make it work,' said Maggie with a smile. And she got straight to it, grabbing some safety pins from her bag to shorten the sleeves and tying the bottom of the shirt in a knot by her hip.

'Looks great, Maggie. You all look great,' said Niki, admiring her team in their shirts and dark jeans. 'PS – who on earth carries safety pins with them? My Maggie the Maker, that's who!'

The guys laughed and so did Maggie. 'I thought the cheer squad might need emergency supplies,' Maggie explained. 'It's best to be prepared.'

Niki checked her watch. 'Speaking of which, the heats start soon. Let's roll.'

They walked for what felt like forever, all the way around to Gate 6, Door 14, Aisle 32. As they ascended the short staircase, the music grew louder until they reached the inside of the stadium.

Taking in the view around them, Maggie's jaw hung open, but Niki's was fixed in a firm smile. She was in awe of the tournament, of course, but found equal happiness in watching Maggie's reactions and sharing the experience together.

'Ha! You can't even manage an "oh my goodness",' said Niki, playfully.

Maggie shook her head. This was something else. The arena looked like a cross between a sporting event and a music concert. There was a massive stage set up in the middle. Ginormous screens were suspended in the air above the stage, so every seat in the house could catch all the action. There were rows of seats on the floor too, and huge lighting rigs flashed in time to the music.

'Feel my hands,' said Maggie nervously, holding her hand out for Niki to touch. 'I can't stop shaking. How on earth am I going to compete with all these people watching?'

Niki looked around – only half of the seats were filled, and the atmosphere was already electric. No wonder Maggie felt nervous. Even Max's cool exterior looked a little shaky.

'You'll smash it,' said Niki as a booming voice came across the speakers.

'Welcome, everyone, to the Castle Capture Cup!'

The crowd cheered as the commentators appeared on the big screens. Niki recognised them instantly. It was Sweeper and PenguinForce, her favourite casters and two of the adult CC champions.

'You are in for one heck of a ride today!' said Sweeper. He was wearing a navy suit and colourful bowtie.

'That's right,' said the woman next to him, as her game name, PenguinForce, appeared across the bottom of the screen. 'Not only will we have the heats and finals of the open age championship, but, for the first time ever, our junior competitors will be hitting the stage!'

The crowd cheered again and Niki felt goosebumps all over her arms.

'The junior heats will commence in ten minutes,' said Sweeper. 'And you'll hear all the action from our commentary team and roving reporters throughout the qualifying rounds!'

Niki and her team made their way down the aisle. At the bottom, an event person scanned their Access All Areas passes and opened the rope so they could walk down to ground level.

'Jupiter!' *CLAP, CLAP, CLAP.* 'Jupiter!' *CLAP, CLAP, CLAP.*

Niki and Maggie spun around to see their cheer squad, complete with pompoms and glow-in-the-dark orange earrings.

'One sec, folks,' said Niki. She grabbed Maggie's hand and hurried along the row of seats to where their friends and family were waiting.

'Look at you!' called Niki as she checked out Hamsa and Eve's outfits. They wore black leggings with orange-and-black tulle skirts. Flashing orange lights had been sewn into the skirts and their orange tops said 'Jupiter FTW' in sparkly black letters. 'Jupiter "for the win"!' said Niki, reading their tops. 'I love it.'

'I can't take any credit,' Hamsa admitted. 'Eve designed the outfits and Maggie made them all.'

'Told you I could add a little bling!' said Maggie, as her mum and stepdad gave her a good-luck kiss.

'And look!' said Hamsa, holding her hands out for Niki to inspect. Her fingernails were painted bright orange with black nail art on top. 'Eve's got the same. They even glow in the dark like our earrings,' Hamsa added proudly.

'Who on earth taught you how to do that?' asked Niki.

Eleni put her hand up, flashing her own matching nail art. 'All that nail polish of mine wasn't so useless after all,' she said with a wink.

Niki laughed and looked at her dad. He managed a smile, although he seemed a little uncomfortable, like he'd arrived at a super-hero birthday party accidentally wearing his footy gear.

'We'll see you after the heats, yeah?' said Niki.

Her dad nodded. 'Good luck . . . and have fun.'

'Thanks,' said Niki.

The butterflies in her tummy were doing cartwheels now. She wasn't even competing but it meant so much to have all her friends and family watching.

'Thanks for coming,' said Niki. 'It means a lot.'

'Don't get all soppy on us,' said Eleni. 'Get out there and win.'

Niki nodded. She steeled herself as she adjusted her coach's hat. 'All right,' she said, her lip curling into a smile. 'Let's do this.'

Chapter 15

If it wasn't for the wizard disappearing dust, Team Jupiter would have been knocked out of the CC Cup in Round 1. Thankfully though, quick-thinking Felix used his ultimate at the exact right time and the jam-packed stadium were on their feet when Magic10 spread the dust across the air, giving her team safe passage through the castle wall.

It was Niki's strategy in Round 2 that got them through. She had prepped the team beforehand to ban Electrica in the draft, which no one saw coming. The semifinal had them win with the narrowest of margins. And now, they were minutes away from entering the grand final against their Round 1 rival, Powerstyde.

By this time there was not a single empty seat in the arena. Even the players from the open age teams were sitting courtside ready to watch the next generation battle.

With her team close by, Niki prepared for her final pep talk. They were standing at the base of the stage and there were a gazillion distractions. Music blared across the speakers, spotlights circled over the crowd and the commentary team analysed every statistic from the earlier matches, live on the big screens.

'Bring it in,' said Niki. She flipped her hat around backwards so they could huddle closely while Maggie's dad and Niki's mum watched on.

'We did it. I knew we could, and we did. *You* did,' Niki corrected herself. She had to shout to be heard over the crowd. 'No matter how well we played in those earlier matches, it means nothing unless we can work together and be present in this match.'

Her teammates nodded, hanging off Niki's every word. After all, she did just coach them into a grand final.

'We're playing Powerstyde again,' said Max, confidently. 'We've beaten them once, we can do it again.'

'Not with that attitude,' Niki corrected him. 'If anything, they'll be more determined than ever to beat us now. And I bet you they'll ban Brutus in the draft. Max, you were awesome playing that character and they won't make the mistake of letting you play him again.'

Max shrugged. He knew Niki was right. 'So what's our strategy then?'

'We think back to our training, and the character book we made. Choose a team that will complement each other. And remember, it's not just about what you see on screen. Behind the characters, us players are all human. We each have strengths and flaws too. And if we can learn from these, we'll be better for it.'

Niki couldn't help but glance at Max. He looked away, giving Niki little hope that he'd ever change.

'From there, it's in your hands,' she went on. 'Try to anticipate what the opposition might do, keep up the great communication and look out for each other.'

'We can do it,' said Archie.

Maggie nodded and smiled nervously.

The crowd cheered, catching the team's attention just as a woman dressed in black jeans, a black t-shirt, and wearing a headset came over. 'You're up,' she said, ushering them towards the stage.

The crowd continued to roar and Niki looked up at the screen, realising the faces of Maggie, Max, Felix and Archie were being beamed right across the stadium.

There was a wide staircase leading up to the stage. While they waited at the bottom, Maggie's dad gave her a quick kiss, which was caught on camera. The crowd *ahhhed*, but she seemed too nervous to be embarrassed by it.

'This team thrilled you in the heats, they won the semifinal in a nail-biter,' said Sweeper, talking down the barrel of the camera. 'Let's welcome them to the stage one last time . . .

it's MegaMax, AstroArchie, FEARlix and Magic10 from JU-PI-TEEEEEEER!'

'Go get 'em!' said Niki, patting her team-mates on the back as they ran up the stairs and onto the stage. When they hit the spotlight the crowd roared even louder. Niki looked back to their cheer squad, holding up signs and swinging their pompoms.

Team Jupiter lined up on stage to one side of the casters.

'Joining them today,' said PenguinForce into her microphone. 'The fierce competitors, ready to take out the first ever Junior Castle Capture Cup, put your hands together for HamBone, Thevan, Dynacraft and Bob from POWERSTYDE!'

The crowd roared again as the opposition ran onto the other side of the stage. One of the players pumped his hands in the air like he was raising the roof.

What a show off, thought Niki, clapping along.

'It's draft time,' said PenguinForce, pulling a coin out of her pocket to flip to see who'd go first. The two team captains stepped forward, while the rest of the players sat down at their computers. Niki's team had chosen Max, given the others were too nervous to speak in front of all those people. The show-off guy, HamBone, was captain for Powerstyde.

'MegaMax, it's your call,' said PenguinForce.

'Tails,' said Max as the coin flipped through the air.

It landed on heads and PenguinForce shook her head. 'Hard luck, Jupiter. We're over to Powerstyde for their first call of the draft.'

HamBone and Max joined their teams, and with no discussion at all, HamBone entered their draft pick on the computer.

The big screens flashed with 'DECISION PENDING' and the crowd waited in anticipation.

'Owwww!' the crowd cooed as an image of Brutus came up on the screen, before being branded with a thick red cross. They must have known what an important play it was.

'Told you,' Niki said to herself.

'Confident choice by HamBone, banning Brutus from the draft without consulting his teammates,' said Sweeper. 'Over to you, MegaMax.'

Max quickly chatted to the team before looking down at Niki. She nodded, willing him along.

Max took a deep breath and made a choice on his computer.

DECISION PENDING flashed again. Then Max's face appeared on the screen and, with a mighty boom from the speakers, his face morphed into Scarlet.

The crowd cheered and the spotlight shone across the stadium finding cosplayers dressed as the iconic sorcerer. Niki wasn't surprised Max chose himself first. She just hoped he hadn't made things difficult for the rest of the team.

'Popular move from Jupiter,' said PenguinForce. 'We have plenty of Scarlet fans in the house.'

The draft continued with Max and HamBone consulting with their teammates, picking and banning until their teams were complete. The music and visual effects on screen were incredible and the crowd went wild with every choice.

'What a spectacle!' said Angela, as she watched the screens. 'I wouldn't be surprised if a hologram of Scarlet appeared in the middle of the stage! I think I like this draft thing.'

Paul agreed. 'I love it. It's like watching the footy draft picks, but better! You get to see the reactions of thousands of people experiencing it together all around you!'

'I don't know anything about that Myke the Mouse, though,' said Angela. 'Is it a good pick for Maggie?'

'Yep. Perfect choice,' said Niki, thinking back to the first time she and Maggie played online together. She took a closer look at her mum and her lip curled into a cheeky grin. 'You've been paying more attention than I thought, Mum.'

Angela shrugged and winked at Niki. 'Maybe a little bit.'

The woman with the headset came past again. 'You'll need to take your seats now,' she said.

Paul led the way to their front row seats. The seat next to Niki had a reserved sign but was still empty. She was so busy watching the stage, she didn't even notice a woman slide into it.

'*Hola, ciao, kon'nichiwa!*'

Niki looked over. 'Yumi! You're here.'

'Yep, *and* I organised front-row seats, *AND* I rigged the seating so I could sit next to you. How are the team feeling?'

'Good, I think. Nervous too.'

'That's standard. I was working during the heats and semifinals, but there was no way I'd miss this match.'

The lights on the audience dimmed and the sixty second countdown appeared on the big screens. It was such a strange feeling for Niki as coach, to put so much energy into something, only for it to be completely out of her hands when it was finally game on. She watched as Max, Maggie, Felix and Archie met in the middle of the stage to shake hands with the opposition. They had one last huddle then took their seats at their computers. Maggie caught Niki's eye. She gave her a small wave and crossed her fingers. Niki held her hands in the air and crossed her fingers too. Or at least she did the best she could with her cast on. She believed in her team. But more than anything, she believed in her friend Maggie.

Further back in the stadium the cheer squad were in full swing. They'd even inspired some of the audience nearby to join them.

'Lucky Maggie packed extra merchandise,' said Eve as she handed orange glow sticks to people in the row behind them. 'We'll have the whole crowd screaming Jupiter by the end of the match!'

Hamsa nodded excitedly. Even Eleni and Niki's dad were swept up in it all.

'I had no idea what was happening with that draft thing,' Hamsa admitted. 'But this is SO! EX! CITING!'

There were just ten seconds left on the clock. By now the entire crowd were chanting the countdown and strobe lights flashed across the stadium roof. Niki wasn't sure what was louder – the crowd or her heartbeat, thumping through her chest. She squeezed her eyes shut as the countdown hit zero. And she couldn't bear to open them until the audience delivered their first big reaction.

She looked up at the screens, seeing that HamBone was off to a great start.

'He's good, that HamBone guy,' said Paul.

Yumi and Niki nodded, too focused to discuss it further.

The match continued, with both teams making small breaks, but neither managing to get ahead.

After fifteen minutes of play, Powerstyde looked like they were finally making progress.

'I feel sick,' said Niki, under her breath.

Mum took her hand, squeezing it tightly. 'There's still time. They can do it.'

But Niki wasn't so sure.

As the game rolled on the cheer squad got better at knowing when to cheer.

'I just listen to the casters when I have no clue what's happening,' Hamsa shouted to

Eve over the noise of the crowd. 'And if all else fails – let's just wave the pompoms!'

Before long, HamBone's character, the little known Antonini, had made it inside the castle, but his teammates were still outside.

'Max, you there?' said Maggie through the headsets. Her fingers were feeling sweaty and swollen, she just hoped they wouldn't slide off the keyboard.

'Yeah,' said Max.

'I think I need to get inside, like I did that first day we played.'

'Really?' asked Archie.

'It's now or never,' insisted Maggie.

'I'm not ready,' Felix butted in. 'I'm still holding back the wizards and if Maggie goes in now, I won't reach her in time.'

The crowd roared as HamBone's character zoomed through the corridors inside the castle.

'You will,' said Max, confidently. His eyes were glued to his computer and his fingers glided across the keyboard. 'We'll have time once HamBone sees Maggie inside.'

Archie shook his head, worried. 'Are you sure, Max? I know we've studied his character Antonini, but we haven't played him much.'

'You're right, I don't know the *character*. But I'm pretty sure I understand the *player*. As soon as HamBone sees the mouse come through that crack in the wall, he'll freak out about looking stupid. He'll panic and make a mistake that'll slow him down. *That's* when we can bust inside.'

'How are you so sure?' asked Maggie.

Max looked away from his screen and smiled at Maggie. 'I hate to admit this,' he said warmly, 'but it's the kind of mistake I'd make.'

Maggie glanced over and caught Max's eye. She smiled back and nodded.

'I've got your back, Maggie. Good luck,' Max said, focusing on his screen again.

Maggie took a deep breath. 'Here goes nothing.'

Chapter **16**

Niki sat in the front row, her hands covering her face. It felt like she'd forgotten to breathe. And she could not stop tapping her foot against the chair leg.

'C'mon, what are they waiting for,' she said to herself. And no sooner had she spoken that Maggie wriggled her way through the crack in the wall.

'What a move from Magic10!' Sweeper's voice boomed across the stadium. He and PenguinForce were giving their live commentary from the side of the stage.

'She is inside the castle! Powerstyde did NOT see that coming!'

'Run, Maggie, run,' said Max through the headsets. 'Just hold your ground and you'll –'

'Whoa! I cannot believe what I'm seeing,' yelled Sweeper. 'HamBone has followed Magic10, getting himself caught in the Wall of Mirrors.

'And Jupiter are seizing on this great opportunity,' PenguinForce added. 'Their players outside are preparing to enter!'

'Hurry!' Niki said to herself. The crowd were deafening. And so was Paul, up on his feet and cheering his little girl on. Even Angela was on the edge of her seat.

'I'm ready with the catapult,' said Archie.

'Nearly there,' said Felix.

'Okay, team, on my call,' said Maggie, carefully watching the screen as Felix's character ran towards the boys. 'Three . . . Two . . .'

Niki jumped to her feet, and her mum and Yumi followed. The seconds felt like hours to Niki and she wished she was wearing a headset so she could hear her team.

'One . . . GO!' shouted Maggie.

The three characters jumped onto the catapult and Archie set it off, shooting them over the castle wall.

The crowd absolutely lost their minds.

'They're in!' called PenguinForce. 'Jupiter soar through space to land inside the castle. It's victory for Jupiter. VICTORY FOR JUPITER!'

BOOM!

Cannons blasted from the corners of the stage, shooting sparkly orange confetti across the crowd.

Team Jupiter were out of their seats, hugging each other and jumping up and down. Meanwhile, on the other side of the stage, the Powerstyde players sat, exhausted and lifeless in their seats, like they'd just run an Olympic relay, only to have one player drop the baton right at the finish line.

'You did it!' said Angela, wrapping Niki in a hug. 'And Maggie. I was so nervous when she was going through the wall. So nervous!'

'Me too,' said Niki and before she knew it, her team were running across the stage and down the stairs to see her, followed by a camera crew.

Maggie led the pack, throwing her arms around Niki. She was so happy, tears were rolling down her checks. 'Niki, we did it! I can't stop shaking!'

Maggie squealed and Niki held her tight as the boys joined them in a group hug. They were under the spotlight and being broadcast live on the big screens.

'Wow, these kids really know how to celebrate!' said PenguinForce, joining Team Jupiter on the floor. 'And it looks like they're not alone . . .'

The camera panned around and Niki looked over her shoulder. The world's best cheer squad were running towards them. Hamsa, Eve and everyone's families.

With pompoms flying in the air, Jupiter shared their win with their favourite people.

'How did you get down here without one of these?' asked Niki, pointing to her Access All Areas pass.

'It's all about who you know,' said Hamsa, cheekily. 'Yumi let us in.'

There were hugs and re-enactments of the best moves in the game while Hamsa was excited to be interviewed by PenguinForce about their costumes and dance moves.

The girls finally managed to steal a moment together, wrapping their arms around each other's shoulders.

'Niki and Maggie, I am so happy for you,' said Eve. 'You killed it out there.'

'Thanks for trusting me to take your spot on the team,' Maggie said to Niki. 'I wish it was you up there. And I so badly wanted to do you proud.'

'You did, Maggie,' said Niki, starting to feel her voice quiver. 'You all did. I don't deserve friends like you.'

'What?' said Hamsa. 'Of course you do.'

Niki shook her head. 'I was ready to give up weeks ago, but you wouldn't let that happen.

I'm so sorry I pushed you away. I'm not good when I'm not in control. I found it really hard to let you help me.'

'Oh, you did? We hadn't noticed,' said Eve, with a smirk on her face.

Niki poked her tongue out at Eve. 'I've realised though, when the four of us get together, there's not much that can stop us.'

'Nothing at all,' said Maggie.

Once things settled down, the casters called Max, Maggie, Archie and Felix back up on stage. Niki stood next to her mum and dad, her arms crossed in front of herself.

'I'm sorry it's not you up there, darling,' said Niki's mum, pulling her in close. 'But you should be so proud of being their coach. I'm proud of you. And so is Dad.'

'Thanks, Mum,' said Niki. And it really meant a lot.

As PenguinForce called out each players name, they met her in the middle of the stage to receive their medals. When the whole team was there, Sweeper handed his microphone over to Max as the team captain.

Max stood, microphone in hand. The crowd were quiet, awaiting his speech. He looked down at the medal around his neck. 'I'd like to get Niki Apostolidis up on the stage,' he said after a while.

The crowd murmured and an unsure applause began, but it was all but washed out for Niki, with Eve and Hamsa standing right beside her screaming their excitement. Before she knew it, the spotlight and cameras had found her in the front row and her face was on the big screen.

She looked up at Max, shaking her head, and he gestured for her to hurry up.

'Go on,' said Hamsa, giving Niki a nudge.

As Niki walked towards the stairs the applause grew.

'I want you all to meet our coach, TrickiNiki,' said Max as Niki crossed the stage to stand with her team.

'She'd earnt her place on this team, fair and square, but an accident stopped her from competing.' Max cleared his throat, like the words were a little stuck. 'You know, I was wrong about Niki. She's the best player I know. She's proven herself as the best coach ever. But above all that, she's an awesome teammate.'

Max looked at his medal thoughtfully, before taking it off.

'Niki, this is yours. You deserve it more than anyone.'

He walked over to Niki, placing the medal around her neck. A heavy lump formed in her throat, and Niki tried desperately to swallow it.

As the crowd cheered she wanted to say thank you, but she didn't know how.

After a while Max leant closer to Niki to be heard over the noise. 'By the way, nice pep talk earlier,' he said with a coy smile.

Niki looked at him and they couldn't help but laugh. 'Whatever,' she said, before giving him a high five.

'Ahhh,' cooed Hamsa, wrapping Eve in a hug as they watched their friend on stage, beaming with pride. 'You know what they say – team work makes the dream work.'

Eve laughed and hugged Hamsa back. 'Yes, Captain Dorksville, they do say that.'

Sweeper walked back to the microphone. 'Unbelievable scenes here for the first ever Junior Castle Capture Cup. Let's hear it one more time for our champions, Team Jupiter!'

The crowd erupted again and the team held hands, lifting their arms up in the air and taking a bow. The confetti cannon went off again.

As they posed for a team photo, holding their medals, Niki could not wipe the smile off her face. Partly because she could see Hamsa and Eve in the corner of her eye, revving the crowd up with their victory dance. But mainly because she was part of a team. And that felt way better than going it alone.

OUR GOAL . . . teach one million women and girls to build the internet by 2025.

Girl Geek Academy is a global movement co-founded by five women in technology – April, Tammy, Lisy, Amanda and Sarah. We are working to increase the number of women with successful technology and games careers. We love to geek out about coding and hackathons, 3D printing and wearables, game development, design, entrepreneurship and startups.

We work with companies, schools and governments to improve their capacity to support women at all stages in the talent pipeline: from teaching young girls to code at age five, right through to getting more women into senior technology leadership roles of large tech companies.

Our programs include hackathons, game jams, school holiday workshops, career incubators, work experience programs and corporate collaborations that make technology careers sustainable, and increase the number of women with professional technical and entrepreneurial skills.

We ask, 'what problem can we solve together?' and we work with you to take action and get it done.

We are women who wanted something like Girl Geek Academy to exist, so we built it. And we'd like you to join us.

For business enquiries, email hello@girlgeekacademy.com

WHAT WOULD THE INTERNET LOOK LIKE IF THERE WERE MORE WOMEN BUILDING IT?

THE GIRL GEEK ACADEMY MANIFESTO

Boldly going where no girl geeks have gone before. There are things to learn, mistakes to make and fun to be had. Where we go, we go together. We support-forward: we are there for each other before we even know we need help.

We sometimes say no: We aren't about being unhealthy, burnt out and undervalued. This means we say no to pizza at meet-ups, crazy long hours for hackathons and not being paid to teach. We celebrate our achievements because they are achievements – not just because they are the achievements of women.

Emojis  welcome

#SheHacksGames

#SheHacksGames is the first all-woman game jam in Australia – and our first hackathon specifically for the gaming industry! We'll match your skills to a team of Girl Geeks and you'll have two days to create a game of any genre and any platform. Along the way we'll fuel you with delicious food, give you access to amazing mentors and at the end, finish with a party to celebrate and share your hard work.

You don't need to have any specific skills to join us, or even have built a game before. Whether you're a programmer, artist/designer or a producer you'll be welcome to play with us!

We've said it before – there is a lack of opportunities for women to develop their skills in the games industry. Our annual #SheMakesGames program became a roaring success, but the feedback was that our community craved more – more hands-on experience, more exposure to the industry and more opportunities to show off what they can do.

#SheHacksGames is perfect for those Girl Geeks who are new or early into their gaming careers and want to spend a weekend letting their creativity, skills and passion run wild to see what they can achieve in a short time. Throw in some great food and great people – you've got yourself a hackathon, Girl Geek Academy style!

#SheMakesGames

You've played games – now hear from the Girl Geeks who make them!

#SheMakesGames is an opportunity to learn and understand the **world of video game development**. It is a great place to start if you've ever been interested in the art of video games.

Maybe you're a **digital marketer** yearning to build a community of game-loving fans or a **graphic designer** who loves building characters.

Believe it or not **your skills are desired in the games industry** – and we're bringing you the best of the best people to share what this amazing world is like!

#MissMakesCode

Did you know Girl Geek Academy CEO, Sarah Moran, started learning coding when she was just five years old? #MissMakesCode is the first initiative in the world created to build confidence and self-efficacy in the areas of algorithmic thinking, programming and coding for young girls aged 5-8 years. This program is available as a one day workshop in schools, a school holiday program at corporate workplaces and as teacher professional development.

And now we also run this program as a gender equality initiative teaching women and girls coding together! The women and girls workshops were first rolled out in January 2019 across Melbourne's East to support mums, daughters, aunts, nieces, grandparents, neighbours and more groups of women and girls to learn coding with each other.

Currently there is a lack of a STEM-based programs that educates both women and girls in the same classroom, and we know the exponential value of working to build intergenerational STEM knowledge. By bringing women and girls together into one workshop, we are able to create something more vital and long-lasting – an instant role model within their immediate family.

By upskilling the women parents and guardians, the girls have a role model in their household who shows confidence and interest in technology, and can work with them on coding games and STEM schoolwork. It could also be an opportunity for the women to explore a new career path option if they wish to cross-skill into this in-demand profession.

#SheHacks

Since 2014 Girl Geek Academy has run #SheHacks – the world's first all-women hackathon. We created #SheHacks to help you make new friends and build a startup together in a weekend. You will find your co-founders and build an MVP – a Minimum Viable Product. We want you to build startups and this is one of the first steps to take.

In 2017 we introduced the #SheHacks Incubator to give women the skills to take their MVP forward to validate, test and build their startup.

With a variety of topics from early customer acquisition through to raising a funding round, this program is designed to provide support and expertise at a time when many startups fall apart.

So work out whether you're a hipster (designer), hacker (developer) or a hustler (marketer/communications/sales) and sign up!

#SheMakes

#SheMakes: the makerfest for Girl Geeks.

Wondering what all this Maker business is about? If you're full of curiosity about 3D printing, wearables and all the things (!) this event introduces basic Making concepts in a friendly way. More advanced Makers also have the opportunity to explore design software and coding, soldering your wearables and messing around with all the 3D printers we have available at these events.

Join us in exploring what it means to be a Girl Geek Maker! Like all of our events, #SheMakes is a great way to learn new skills, test new business ideas and meet new people to build things with.

Thank You!

We love hearing from people who share our passion
for all things Girl Geek.

If you want to get in touch simply email us at
hi@girlgeekacademy.com

Read on for an extract
from the first book in the
Girl Geeks series

The Hackathon

Chapter 1

'One spot for Sal, who's the trendiest gal. One for Wai-Ling, who can swim, run and sing . . .'

Hamsa recited the poem she'd made up as she placed books around the table, reserving the seats for her best friends. It was before school and kids were starting to file into the classroom.

'One for Michelle, who plays handball so well. One for Zo-eeeee, who can sit next to me. And lucky-last Hamsa, who's . . .' *Hmmmm*, thought Hamsa. She always got stuck at that point of her poem.

She carefully placed her pencil case in front of her, sat down and tucked her short dark hair behind her ears. The trouble was that Hamsa didn't think she was particularly good at anything. But 'not particularly good' didn't rhyme with 'Hamsa' anyway.

From her table near the window, Hamsa looked around the room. Her friends hadn't arrived yet, but she did see someone new standing in the doorway. She was tall, had black hair pulled back in a messy bun and her uniform looked brand-spanking new. Hamsa watched as the girl made her way to an empty table.

Just as Hamsa was about to invite her to come over:

BANG!

The girl tripped and went crashing to the floor. Her books and pencil case flew out of her arms. When she looked up all the kids were staring at her.

'I am SO sorry!' called Niki, rushing over.

'So you should be!' said Hamsa, joining them and helping the new girl to her feet. 'There's a reason Ms Atlas says to leave that stupid thing outside.'

Hamsa pointed to the cause of the accident. It was Niki's well-travelled skateboard, painted black with colourful stickers covering the artwork underneath.

'It's not stupid, but sure, I'll take it out.' Niki stepped on one end of the board, flicking the other end up in the air. She caught it casually by her side. 'I really am sorry. Are you okay?'

The new girl nodded while Hamsa took her hand. 'You're just being polite. I bet you're not okay. I bet you're hurt and you'd one hundred per cent be embarrassed. But if it makes you feel better, I do embarrassing things *all* the time.'

Niki rolled her eyes and walked off while Hamsa leant in close.

'Last week,' she whispered, 'I went to the loo at lunchtime and tucked my dress into my undies by accident. None of my friends told me when I came out. It wasn't until the kids in Grade 1 started yelling "Look at that unicorn bum!" that I realised.'

'Unicorns?!' the girl asked, giggling. She had a hint of an accent, but Hamsa couldn't place where it was from.

'Yeah, I had unicorns on my undies. It's dumb and childish, I know, and by Grade 5 you should totally be over unicorns, but I think they're so awesome! Oh gosh, now I've just told you how much I love unicorns and you're going to think I'm dumb too. Are my cheeks as red as yours were? I bet they are.'

'I don't think you're dumb.' The girl smiled. 'My name's Eve Lee, by the way.'

'I'm Hamsa Pillai. It's great to meet you.'

'Excuse me,' said a small voice. It belonged to a girl with a pristine school dress, round silver glasses and neatly braided blonde hair. She was holding Eve's pencil case.

She shyly handed it back.

'Thanks,' said Eve.

The girl smiled before hurrying away.

'Who's that?' asked Eve, as Hamsa led her back to their table.

'That's Maggie Milsom. She doesn't say much, but she does make the most amazing crochet cats.'

'Cats?' asked Eve.

'Or any toy animals really. You should see her knitting and crocheting at lunchtime. Her fingers move so fast.' Hamsa pointed to the next table along. 'That's Ezra. He broke his leg last term. And Katherine, she always has the best lunches.'

'What about that girl with the skateboard?' asked Eve. 'She seems nice . . . but in a you-better-not-mess-with-me way.'

'That's Nikoleta Apostolidis. We all call her Niki. And you're spot-on,' said Hamsa, watching Niki sit down at a table on her own. 'It's like she's friends with everyone and no one at the same time, and she doesn't seem to mind. This is the first year we've been in a class together, so I hardly know her, except that she skates and is into gaming.'

The truth was, Hamsa had never tried to get to know Niki. Her confidence was kind of intimidating.

Eve nodded and Hamsa surveyed the room, looking for other interesting facts to share with the newbie. She was excited to have a potential new friend, but was also trying her best to give a good first impression. Eve covered her mouth as she tried to hold back a yawn.

'Oh gosh, I'm boring you already,' said Hamsa, worried.

'Not at all,' said Eve. 'It's the jetlag. I've only been in the country for three days.'

'So that's why you're starting school in the middle of Term 2?'

'Yep,' said Eve.

'And you've flown in from . . .?'

'San Francisco, in the States. We moved there are few years ago for my dad's work, but now we're back in Australia. I've moved around quite a lot.'

'Wowsers, we're like total opposites. I've been in the same house my whole life. Although I did get to move bedrooms when my little brothers were born. I have four of them.'

'Four bedrooms?' asked Eve.

'I wish!' said Hamsa. 'No, brothers. Two older and twins who are younger. And they're so stinky when they're all together. Worse than pickled dog food left in the sun for weeks.'

'Whoa. Major stink,' agreed Eve. 'It's just me and Dad in my house. And I don't think we smell too bad.'

'Well, I wasn't going to say anything, but . . .' Hamsa waved her hand in front of her nose, and the girls couldn't help but laugh. When Hamsa noticed something over Eve's shoulder, her face lit up. 'Here come my friends. I'll introduce you.'

The group made their way over. 'Everyone, this is Eve,' said Hamsa proudly. 'She's new *and* she's from America!'

'I'm actually Aussie. I've just been living over there for a few years,' said Eve.

'Hi, I'm Zoe,' said one of the girls taking a seat. The others joined her. 'This is Sal, Michelle and Wai-Ling. You should sit with us today.'

'Thanks,' said Eve, and Hamsa winked at her.

'See,' said Hamsa. 'You'll be feeling right at home in no time.'

As they waited for their teacher to arrive, Hamsa admired Eve's workbooks, each covered with detailed drawings. It wasn't every day that *she* was the one to show the rest of her friends something (or someone) special.